The President's Life

Murl Edward Gwynn

The President's Life (Originally published as The President Was A Good Man - Copyright 2009 © Murl Gwynn)

Copyright 2013 © Murl Gwynn

ISBN: 978-0-9711766-5-2

Printed in the United States of America

MEG Enterprises Publication, PO Box 2165, Reidsville, GA 30453

To Ruth!

Chapter

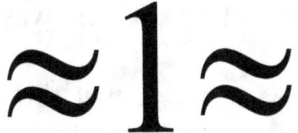

The sardonic laughter of the unseen beings could be heard just above the fading echoes of gun shots. Although their form could not be realized in the small, one bulb lit room, they were there nevertheless. After the shots that ripped through flesh, shattered bone, and ended a life, the demons were pleased with their convincing demands on open minds of madness.

The President had been shot. Some crazy religious nut was the rumor that was going around. This guy thought he was doing God a favor by getting rid of the most hated President in the history of the United States. President Jack Prinston's body was found with four bullets in it, one in his head, one in his mouth, one in his right hand, and the other in his heart.

How America had gotten to this point in their history was beyond many people's thinking. The prosperity index was so far ahead of any projections that there were no poor, sick or hungry. Everyone that could work or wanted to worked. There was no pollution, illegal drugs, or open sexual display anywhere, and people generally obeyed the law. You would have thought on that bright spring day with the birds chirping and flowers blooming that we, as a people, had arrived.

Why would someone want to kill the President? So many people hated him, not because he was corrupt, or led the country with a strong arm, but because he was a "good man."

A good man in the eyes of the world at that time was one who let everyone do his or her own thing. Doing your own thing was legal, accepted, and almost demanded in the society that had all but forgotten the difference between good and evil. Good was anything that made you feel good, happy, and uplifted. Evil was anything that made you feel just the opposite; therefore, as long as you did not hurt anyone else, it was good.

Jack Prinston had been the President for five years and had won his second presidential election with a landslide victory of 68 percent of the voters. The only ones that did not vote for him were those who never voted and a few disgruntled party-line hold-ons. The population had loved his wife, and his children were the darlings of the nation.

So, what had turned the people of the great nation into haters of the President? I guess to answer that question we have to go back to the year 2030 when he was first voted into office by a 48 percent victory.

In 2030 people were tired of politicians who said one thing but did another. Corruption was rampant and everyone was poor, tired and sick. The populace was looking for change in its leaders, but unwilling to change themselves. Everyone wanted his or her share of the American dream but without the responsibility that went with it. Jack Prinston was no different; he was a typical son of the nation. He loved women, money, and the high life. It didn't matter to him who knew his lifestyle and corrupt ways of thinking and he told the truth.

Now how could a corrupt politician tell the truth? He told the truth about everything he did; he just did his corruption openly. He told people what he wanted, why he wanted it, and how he would get it. Jack's life was an open book for all to read. He became the nation's little rascal of politics, and the more he did, the more he was liked, accepted, and expected to do. As long as he didn't openly hurt anyone and shared the "goods" with as many people as possible he was a winner in the voters' eyes.

His wife Nora laughed at his shenanigans and loved him no matter what he did. Her life was not as open as Jack's, and she had secrets that would one day be published. Nora supported everything Jack did because she was proud that her husband and would be president was not a hypocrite. They belonged to each other and truly loved each other's company. In a sense, they were two peas in a pod.

Nora was very attractive and carried herself with grace and dignity. Her slender five nine build, long legs, and striking figure always caught the eyes of men. She was a golden blond beauty but wasn't the typical stereo type of the dumb blond. Her mind was sharp, and she could hold her own within the political world. Jack could speak with her about any topic from foreign affairs to budget matters, and Nora would have something of worth that he could use to govern. She was no dummy!

As the First Lady, Nora proved to be an asset to the nation. She often put visiting dignitaries at ease and could speak in five languages, which helped to insure success in negotiations.

The Prinston children, Nathan and Rebecca, were as opposite in nature as a dove and a wild cat. Nathan was a gentle soul who loved people, hated wrong and was always the peacemaker. He was easy going but had a touch of lazy in him. Being raised the way he was and the son of the President, he had it made for doing little and sitting back. It wasn't that he couldn't be more industrious, it just came easy.

Rebecca loved the nightlife, sex, booze and the trappings of darkness. Her short and dumpy physical makeup did not do her well in the setting of the White House or that of a President's daughter. It was probably because she didn't feel accepted by people that she leaned toward the darker side of life. She loved anything that was weird and a little off center. Nathan was always trying to calm his sister down, but she would have none of his temperament or calm lifestyle.

Neither Jack nor Nora took time with their children and left it up to nature, age, and circumstance to teach them the basic principles of life. Their children were smart, curious, and open to new ideas, one with the innocence of a baby and the other with the cunning mentality of a pit viper. Nathan's personality came by nature, but Rebecca's was molded by neglect and influences of spiritual darkness through her mother's associations.

In time Jack would come to regret his wayward lifestyle and lack of parental input into his children's lives. As intelligent as Nora was, she would see but not understand, hear but not comprehend, and converse without any thought of proper perception of adult supervision. Such was the Prinston home.

*

Stepping up to face Supreme Court Justice William Matthews was a dream come true for Jack Prinston, and his children were the last thing on his mind. The day was cool, calm, bright, and with a touch of nostalgia that was orchestrated by Jack's personal touch on taking the oath of office of the President of the United State.

He wore a black top hat, tailored tux with tails, perfectly groomed mustache grown just for the occasion because he wanted to look like his hero politicians from the 1920's and 30's. He insured that he had his yellow ribbons for the many Aids patients that had died in the past and a white carnation in place upon his chest. He was the well dressed, soon to be President on that January morning. His six foot frame and football style physique were very impressive as he stood there that inauguration day.

As he said "I do" to complete the oath of office (the "So help me God" had been dropped many years before), he declared, "And we will have fun doing it!"

The crowds present and everyone throughout the country watching on T.V. laughed and shouted for joy with the new president they saw as one of them.

You would have to admit, it was a fun time in the USA that year. The new President said all the right things and had a cabinet of professionals that sounded too good to be true. His platform of reforms was sound and capable of being carried through Congress. If the politicians would go along with his fast paced way of doing things he would bring the country to prosperity in a short time.

Chapter

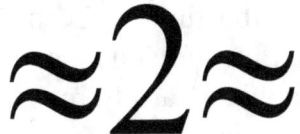

President Prinston settled into the oval office, satisfied that his staff was performing to his sick standards. His method of leadership was to keep people guessing who the office snitch was, making sure that everyone suspected everyone else.

Vice President John Lambkin was a "yes man" and did exactly what he was told. In no case would he make a decision without the consent of President Prinston. He was a loyal man and truly wanted to see the country prosper. People were important to him and the means never justified the end if it hurt them.

Chief of Staff Richard Merrill was a brilliant individual who found a joke in anything. He was tough on the staff, but could find time to laugh, make a joke, and stop to smell the flowers throughout the day. His wife loved Washington as well as being known as Mrs. Merrill.

President Prinston's personal secretary, Jane Dean, was a petite quick-witted individual that didn't have time for nonsense or laziness. She, like most of the women in Jack Prinston's life, was a beauty. Her talents were many, and she often gave advice that worked. She also had an eye for her boss. He made her his personal secretary because he knew her father and had learned of her skills through invitations to the Dean home. Jane had masters degrees in Political Science, History, and Social Science. Her secretarial skills were matchless, and taking the time to be the president's personal secretary was fun and done just to help. She put her own career on hold to learn from one of the best politicians in the country, Jack Prinston.

In President Prinston's first 100 days in office he passed through more bills strengthening the country than any other President in history. One day he would mention a topic, bill, or piece of legislation, and within a few weeks it would become law. It was no wonder that the prosperity level in the country grew so quickly. Wall Street loved him and corporate America trusted his judgment. His business knowledge was sound, aggressive, and stable. What he proposed worked.

How he pulled off his amazing pieces of legislative magic was another thing, however. You see, he had anybody who was somebody in his pocket. He knew the dirty secrets of every person on Capital Hill and then some. Those who didn't have a dark envelope of human weaknesses could be wooed with the charm of a loved lost one.

Corporate America loved him. They would go along with his "suggestions" because they trusted him and were up to the challenge to try something new. Like the time he called all of the top executives from the major corporations together. He had something radical he wanted to try and if successful, it would bring unprecedented prosperity for the nation, as well as those CEOs.

The crowd of top brass billionaires from the manufacturing, press, entertainment, services, and media in the White House Dining Room that day was most impressive to say the least. They all arrived willing to listen, extend a hand of cooperation, and experiment with the nation's financial future.

President Prinston started with his usual jokes, warm slaps on the backs and glad-handing. When he got down to business, he was serious, firm, and very persuasive. "Ladies and Gentlemen, I am so very delighted to have you with me today. Thank you so very much for accepting my invitation. I know that most of you are unsure why I asked you here. However, if you will open your hearts and minds to what I am going to propose to you, I am sure we will realize a mutual benefit from this meeting and future endeavors together. What I am about to propose is so radical that it may scare some of you, but I can assure you I am serious and I am sure it will work."

The room became as quiet as church on Monday. Everyone was looking around to get an indication if anyone knew what was going on. Someone coughed, and it made others jump; it was that quiet in the room. The President continued.

"I am asking that each of your companies stop advertising in all forms for one year!" *One year! Was he crazy? After all, advertising was what drew people to their products and services. Without advertising how would people hear?*

"Yes, I said stop advertising for one year. Within that year I would ask that you give the amount of money you would have spent on advertising to disease research, alternate sources of energy research and social betterment." If the room was quiet before, it was now vacant of even human brain waves, as this suggestion made the minds of the power base in the country warp into never-never-land.

"Now, I know some of you are perplexed as to this request." President Prinston went on.

"But I can assure you I have thought through this radical approach to our country's financial and social situation very carefully. Here's how it will work. If you will take the money you would have put into advertising and give it to the research I have suggested, your name will be on every institution, and product that comes out of that research. Your advertising will just be attached to the research instead of advertising for advertising sake. I am calling this plan 'Un-Ad.'"

The CEO of CBS stood to his feet and asked, "What will that do to our financial base if we can not receive funds we charge for advertising?" President Prinston did not look concerned by this question as he responded. "Well, you will open the advertising airways at a lower price to local and regional business. Instead of large accounts, you will have many smaller accounts. They will be the advertising base for the companies and services. With the lower prices you charge, the local and regional businesses will be able to pay the advertising prices without the corporate subsidies." CBS as well as the other media people seemed to accept that answer.

Each in their turn had questions as to how their particular business would be affected, and received the same common sense answers and assurances that just made it seem so right.

"Manufacturing, your products will sell themselves because your name will be associated with each research project, and when the press and media advertising elements mention the research project, your name will be attached. Sure, there may be instances that will fall through the cracks, but what the hey, this is for research and the betterment of our nation. Entertainment, everything you produce will have project research attached to it. It doesn't cost you anything to mention the research or the companies that are involved anyway. Service companies, your advertisement will come from word of mouth in local areas and the free ads given by local media."

It all sounded a little crazy, but for some reason those present went along with it. In about a month, the plan had been hatched, with a lot of help from the President's staff and a little prodding by his secret deals on dark nights. Jack Prinston had so many markers out that he could call anyone at anytime and close a deal without much fanfare or resistance. And call in markers he did.

President Prinston took almost every weekend during his first year in office for a get-away at Camp David. During those get-a-ways he would invite two or three people who "owed" him and then put the strong arm on them. In every case they would come around to Jack's way of thinking. It was not that they were afraid or embarrassed for their hidden past; it was because they were concerned about losing money or even their jobs because of the deals they had made that had hurt others.

"Un-Ad" worked to a tee. Money was pouring into research faster than anyone would have imagined. Within the second year from the start of "Un-Ad" Aids, Alzheimer's, most major causes of heart problems, children's sicknesses, and many other well known sicknesses had been conquered. Because the "Un-Ad" became so popular, other businesses stopped advertising altogether. The pornographic industry stopped their ads openly and no longer printed material to be sold over the public counters. This material was still available, but only in so-called private clubs, which had sprung up everywhere. There were so many clubs that there was no need to advertise openly. It was looking like society was cleaning its act up, but in reality, it was becoming more morally corrupt without the open advertising of its dirty details.

Within another year the unemployment rate was one percent. There was so much research going on that those who had lost their jobs because of less advertising found work in research. Institution after institution was building, expanding and exploring new avenues of doing things.

Alternate sources of energy research came up with a perfect fuel cell that was as small as a one-suit suitcase. It could power an entire house and if operated properly could put energy back into the electric grid. On a smaller scale the cell could also power a full sized automobile for 1,125 miles.

Needless to say, fossil fuels went to other things, and smog was a thing of the past.

Social research finally got everyone's ear by proclaiming, "If big companies can be in unity so can individuals!" Everyone got on board the unity wagon. Cooperation was the by-word of the day. People were volunteering for all kinds of public, private, and corporate social needs.

Although the family was no stronger than before, it had the appearance of unity. Unity in this case was that everyone just did what they wanted, without hurting others. The effect on individuals without restraint, however, made for a lot of lonely, confused children.

You can imagine what the country thought of the man who had the idea that brought them prosperity.

——————— * ———————

Jane Dean was so enamored by her boss, the President, she was beside herself. She was the envy of all her girl friends, and they treated her like a queen. When she went into his office for dictation or some other task, she always made sure she had a reason to reach over the desk or adjust something on it in order to just touch or rub his person. He understood and knew her intentions.

One day, as usual, when Jane had gone through her routine of dictation, reaching, touching and looking, Jack touched her hand and caressed it. She looked at him with a soft, calling, howbeit shy smile, walked around the desk and sat in his lap. Jack didn't say a word but kissed her passionately while she responded.

That was the beginning of their new relationship. Most nights when Jack was not working or away on State trips, he was with Jane. Nora knew it and didn't care, as she had her own life, but she still loved Jack in her own sick way. Jane, however, thought that Jack loved only her.

*

Vice President Lambkin was swept off his feet by the fast paced lifestyle and work of the new President. He was out of his element, but wouldn't do anything to bring attention to his inadequacies. He said yes to just about everything the President wanted to do and insured that every request and whim was carried out. Although he agreed to be Jack Prinston's running mate because he was the Party's soundest mind, he didn't like Jack personally. To him, Jack was an opportunist, one who would cut your throat if you gave him a chance. He was right! He also knew that Jack knew his dark secrets and had to kowtow or be exposed. Kowtow he did, and soon became a master at it to the point that he loathed himself and Jack Prinston.

*

Chief of Staff Richard Merrill, as would be expected, carried out the business of the President's staff with utmost proficiency. He had the President's ear on any subject and could interject any idea, topic or problem without any fear. He had known Jack from high school and they were friends. They were friends enough to share everything while growing up and as adults. They shared cars, funds, food, and women. It would be the latter that would be Richard's undoing with his friend. Nora, you see, had been Richard's girl friend during college, but she saw Jack's potential for the White House even then and soon dumped Richard for Jack. Richard pretended to get over it, but he didn't. He held this one chip of valuable memory for a later game of human poker. He knew that one day he could use it against Jack and win back Nora. Or so he thought!

*

Rebecca Prinston, now in her late twenties, loved being the President's daughter. Living in the White House with Daddy only added to her inflated ego, and she acted the part. She couldn't hold down a job because of her weird personality and, therefore, stayed home in the White House. Most of the White House staff hated her to the same degree that the unknowing public loved her. The public saw her as a darling and the staff saw her as a demon. The demon in her caused her to act, and react, in some of the most bizarre ways imaginable.

Rebecca, on one occasion, while walking down the steps from the family quarters, jumped upon the back of a cleaning maid, Wannetta Morales. Screaming at the maid, pounding her on the back, Rebecca belched out, "I know who you are! Stop looking at me and accusing me with your thoughts!" The maid, frightened, went running down the stairs and out the front door praying, "Gloria a' Dios, Jesús, salvo mío!" or "Glory to God, Jesus help me!"

---- * ----

Nathan Prinston, now in his early twenties, did not have an ego problem and took living in the White House as neat, but nothing so great. He didn't like having to be surrounded by Secret Service agents every place he went. He was polite, warm, and had time for anyone. There was a cool, calm, collected air about him that just seemed to say, "You are accepted around me!" People loved to talk with him because he made them feel special.

---- * ----

Nora Prinston enjoyed being the President's wife. The power she gained by being the First Lady opened up to her people and things that fed her soul, but choked her spirit. She was by no means a religious person, but found that the more she let the power over people manifest itself the lower she felt inside. Fighting those feelings caused her to call upon mediums and search out dark forces to find relief. She never did.

On one occasion while sitting through a medium's session, the table moved and the lights flickered; she felt something like a cold hand upon her throat. She never went back to that medium, but tried others and continued to read books and dig into the occult.

Chapter

The stage had been set for a tragedy, a President who was loved by the nation, but not by those who knew him personally, a First Lady who probably was under the covert influence of demons, a daughter who was demon possessed, a son who was open for truth and change, and a staff that probably would do anything to keep from being exposed, ridiculed and brought low.

Across Washington, D.C., things were taking place that would affect the nation by pure chance. Chance?

---- * ----

Albert Frank was a good, clean cut, Christian man and father of three with a loving wife, Delores.

Delores was a typical housewife of the twentieth century and 1950's and she didn't fit into the modern fast passed times. She was not a New Age thinker and she really enjoyed being a stay-at-home mom.

Albert was a plumber by trade, but a would-be preacher at heart. He spent his nights with his family and found time to read and study his Bible. Being a plumber supplied his family with just about everything they wanted without any extravagances. They were happy!

"Delores, do you know where I put that advertisement about the new plumbing company in the city?"

"No, dear, I think you were looking at it in the den last night, however. Why? Are you thinking about going to work with them?"

"I don't know. Jeff Baughman told me that they would be paying almost twice the going rate for hired plumbers associated with them. I may check it out!"

"Don't forget, Albert, you promised the children that you would take them on a tour of the White House today!"

"I haven't forgotten. We'll be leaving at one!"

---
*

Nora sat in the semi dark Lincolns bedroom with her newest medium, Madam Welslie. Welslie was no ordinary medium, as she was known for her accuracy and many strange happenings that followed her. She spoke softly, with unblinking hazel eyes that looked like they came from a snake's corpse rather than a breathing human. She would make the average person shiver with concern, but not Nora. Nora wanted to know her future and gain more power and control.

Madam Welslie started the session with a short prayer. Now this prayer was not to any god in particular, but rather to any deity that would listen. She prayed, "Forces of strength and power, 'Knowing One' who is there. We ask for your presence and ability to show us that you care. Come and give insight, wisdom, and knowledge. Direct this seeker, Nora Prinston, in her quest to please you and do your bidding." Nora sat still, nerved and yearning for something that could give her peace as well as more power and fulfillment. What she didn't know was that she would be immersed into the insanity of a dreamlike state that would control her emotions and demand satisfaction of its own.

Nora spoke after Madam Welslie, "God of this time and place, come and reveal yourself. Help me to know you and do your bidding. Thank you!" She then added, "I give you my life!"

Just then there was a low rumbling someplace within the White House. It was a strange groaning, kind of like the one you hear when a dog or lion would stretch itself. Every person in the building could hear it, and in some cases they could feel it pass through their bodies like a wave of liquid darkness. Some even felt wheezy and had to run to the bathrooms.

*

Albert, Deloris and their children made their way across Washington for their first tour of the White House. Although they had lived in the Nation's capital city for ten years, they had never taken the time to see this historic site. Albert took the long way around instead of going directly to the parking area for White House tours. He took the family down one historic street then the other. Past the monuments of Washington, Lincoln, Jefferson, the Smithsonian buildings, the Capital buildings, Supreme Court and then the Treasury, and at each junction and street he gave a brief history. The children loved it and looked at their father with much love and trust. By the time they arrived at the parking lot, the gates were being opened for tours.

"Hurry up children; we don't want to be late as this is the last tour of the day!"

"Maybe we will see the President or some other important person," said his youngest with a smile of anticipation.

"Maybe, but remember what I told you; don't touch anything, and try to keep quiet as we listen to the tour guide!"

"Yes, Dad!"

The Franks, along with the other tourists, had left one room and entered the next on the tour. "This is the 'China Room,' as it contains every patterned dish ever created to be used for special state dinners." The tour guide knew her stuff and made you feel like visiting the most important building in the nation was by special request only for you. Just then, from somewhere, everywhere in the White House, you could hear the groaning. It sounded like a lion, or more aptly, like a lion that was stretching. People looked visibly shaken. Some asked for a bathroom, and others looked around for some unseen support.

Water came rushing out of the wall and looked like it would flood the room. It gushed from the south wall, and its force knocked some people off their feet. After the initial shock, the tour guide directed everyone down and out of the building. In her haste, however, she only took the people to just outside the front door instead of off the property. Everyone stood there, mingling about waiting for direction.

"Turn the water off!" spoke a demanding voice from within the building.

"I don't know where the shut off valve is!"

"Where is the groundskeeper or plumber?"

"They have been given three days off, and the fill-in is sick." No one seemed to know what to do. You would think that somebody would have taken charge, but no, this was a problem that had not been anticipated. So what if the plumber would be away?

"Excuse me, I am a plumber!" interrupted Albert Frank. "Can I help?"

A Secret Service agent standing there spoke up, "Yes, come with me!" At that, Albert Frank was ushered back into the White House and into an adventure that would demand everything of Christian upbringing and will power. His family was told that he would be late and that they could leave. Deloris took the children, drove home and waited for word from her husband.

Albert was led down corridors past stored furniture and walked through musty dank cubbyholes. The Secret Agent took him to any place they could think of that would control the water pipes in the China Room.

"Do you have building blue prints of the White House?" asked Albert as he took in this special house and its property.

"Yes in the main Agents' room."

"We will need it." said Albert.

"Come with me." said the agent, and off they went to get the print. When they arrived, the agent gave Albert a "Workers Pass," which let him go into any room within the White House. It was needed for security reasons and the one they gave him was for the entire complex. Albert, in essence, had just been given the "run of the grounds." He could go wherever he wanted or needed to.

As the agent gave the building blue prints to Albert the phone rang. "Agent Whitaker! Yes, yes, I will be right there!"

"I have to leave you. Do whatever you have to do to stop that water. I will meet up with you as soon as I can." At that, the agent was gone and Albert was left alone with the blue print, his pass, and his thoughts. *"Where to begin?"*

He soon found the main line that directed water past the China Room, but it was close to the stairway leading up to the family quarters. He grabbed wrenches and rags and ran back in the direction he and the agent had come, almost hitting the furniture, but too quickly to smell the mildew and musty orders of the cubbyholes. As he ran, sometimes walking, he continued glancing at the blue print, but he was not always aware of his surroundings. It was just up the last flight of stairs, as he turned the corner that he hit someone face on.

Down they both went, Albert reeling toward one wall and the unsuspecting other person to the adjacent wall. "Wop!" went the poor soul who had been hit by Albert Frank, two hundred and forty five pound six footer. All you could hear were thuds, air being passed out of lungs and mournful cries of, "OHHHHH!"

"I am so sorry, I hope I didn't hurt you." was all Albert could say as he slowly picked himself up and turned to see who it was. It was the President of the United States. All Albert could say was, "Oh no!"

Secret Agents were all over Albert as he just stood there gawking at the President.

"I am so sorry, sir!" said Albert.

"Who in this world are you?" said the President.

"I am Albert Frank, sir. A plumber! I was asked to help stop the water flow coming out of the wall in the China Room."

"Good on you, man. Forget about the little mishap. What do you think caused the leak?"

"I don't know, sir, but I am going to give it my best to get it stopped."

The President looked at Albert, surmised that he was a man of purpose and determination and said, "Let's go fix that pipe!"

Albert was surprised with the President's adventuresome attitude, but led the way. Here they were a little group of searching water explorers, some with suits, guns, walky-talkies and others with wrenches and rags. The President knew a short cut to the possible affected area, all the while talking about plumbing problems. Apparently he had been a plumber's helper as a youth and this mishap brought back memories that would not be suppressed. Besides, the President liked to do things with his hands.

As they approached the now water logged carpeted area, Albert could see the little trap door that contained the shutoff valve. He opened it, looked in, and reached for the valve, but his hand froze in place. The valve looked fine and workable, but the surrounding area and pipes looked like they had melted into a soft, gooey, mess of spaghetti. Above the valve and toward the main area of the problem was a plaque that read "Shutoff-China Room." Just above the plaque was a hand written card, that some worker had put there when the water pipes were installed in the building that read "Blessing to this House. May God bring His will through this place as freely as water flows through these pipes!"

Albert, being a Christian, was touched by the "Blessing" and moved by the now gone to glory saint who had put it there. He reached in and turned the valve, and the water stopped. "Look here, Mr. President, what do you make of that?" Albert said. The President looked at the mess and noticed the plaque, but did not see the card. All he could see were the gooey pipes and their weird configuration. One of the Secret Agents said, "What a mess! I bet it will take a lot of PVC pipe to replace that mess."

Albert and the President responded together, "No way! You don't use PVC pipe in that kind of plumbing. It would never last. It will have to be replaced with copper."

They turned to each other and laughed. The President said, "Great minds think alike!" He put his arm around Albert and said, "How about some coffee?"

*

Nora and Madam Welslie sat stunned. They both had felt some entity enter the room, linger for a moment and then depart in the direction down toward the China Room. Although they had not known what had happened, they felt like their "Prayer" had been answered. Neither of the searchers knew what they had brought into the White House and what it would do. They just knew that they were in touch with some unseen power, which they thought was for good. They were wrong!

Nora could not sleep normally after the China Room incident. She would wake up in the middle of the night in a cold sweat, sensing a presence in the room that wanted her. Many nights she would walk the corridors of the White House, looking for something she felt like she had lost. She was a troubled soul.

On the night of the China Room incident she wandered here and there, looking for Jack to comfort her. When she did find him it was in the Blue Room on a couch with Jane Dean. They pretended to be only talking, but Nora knew from their surprise and composure that there was more going on than business. It made her skin crawl thinking that Jack cared more about Jane than his hurting wife after the kind of day she had just had. It was the beginning of hate in her heart toward Jack.

Chapter

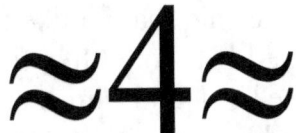

When Albert got home, he was ecstatic. "Well, tell us everything!" Deloris queried before he even had time to get in the door and sit down.

"Let me catch my breath! Man, you just never know what is in store for you. Just a simple tour, and, bam, there you are in the middle of a crisis and then a whole new direction for your life."

"What, what, honey, what happened, what about a changed life, what?" Deloris inquired, noticeably catching the excitement in Albert's story.

"Well, you are now looking at the new 'Plumber's Helper of the White House'!"

"Plumber's Helper, White House, how, what, why?" squealed Deloris with the children jumping around.

"OK, everybody sit down, and I will tell you the story!"

After Albert finished telling about knocking down the President, the melted pipes, and the hand written card, he was exhausted with joy. "And, there we were, walking down the corridor with the President's arm around my shoulder, going for coffee. Just like two old buddies!"

"Oh, come on Albert, you have got to be kidding us?" declared Deloris. "Arm around your shoulder?"

"Yes, dear, and not only that, he said that he liked the way I handled myself and asked if I would like to be a plumber at the White House?" I told him that they probably had one already, and he said, "If we do, we will make you a plumber's helper!'"

"I said yes!"

"How wonderful, Albert!" said Deloris. "Does it pay well?"

"Yes, you little money grubber, it pays triple what I am making now!" With that, Deloris sat down, turned ashen white, and began to fan herself.

"I start to work at the 'House' in one week!" said Albert, thumbs in his armpits, and head held back.

"Now, Albert, you know what pride can do. You'd better thank God for that job!"

"I do, I do, and I have done nothing but since I left there this evening. 'Thank you, Jesus'!"

———————— * ————————

A few days pass.

———————— * ————————

Vice President Lambkin could barely keep up with all of the reports, senate bills, and his executive schedule. He was in and out of the President's office many times throughout the day, asking questions, needing advice, and generally trying to find his place. The President was becoming totally annoyed by him, and a show down was in the making.

"The Vice President to see you again, sir!" Jane Dean informed the President, with her head in the door as she winked.

"Man, what am I going to do with this guy? Send him in, again!"

"Mr. President, I'm sorry to disturb you again, but I just need to ask you about Senate Bill 6116!"

"Yes, what about it?"

"Well, sir, there is this rather odd comment on a slip of paper attached to the bill that was sent to me. I think it was supposed to go to you, but I got it instead." Reaching across the desk, flipping his hand in a come here jester, President Prinston was visibly disturbed.

"What does it say? Let me see it!"

"Sir, I don't understand what the note meant by, 'Green paper will be sent to the proper account when passed'!"

Jack tried to show no concern, but you could tell that the note affected him, deeply.

"I guess it was some clerk just writing down a reminder note about what to do when Bill 6116 is passed. You know, these young clerks don't want to make any mistakes."

"But, sir, shouldn't we check this out, in case there is an impropriety here?"

"No!" demanded Jack, but caught himself and softened quickly.

"But, sir!" said Lambkin. At that, President Prinston stood to his feet, walked around the desk, laid his hand on the Vice President's shoulder and patted him condescendingly, stating, "Don't worry your little head over it, now!"

John Lambkin was a yes man, but he could not stand someone condescending to him. He stood to his feet and blurted out "Now see here, Jack, don't treat me like a child! I think you know what that note meant, and I want to know!"

"I know we are friends and mates, John, but don't forget who you are talking to!" Jack superiorly pontificated. The Vice President looked surprised, beaten, but underneath was boiling.

"If that's the way it's going to be from now on, so be it, 'Mr. President'!'" and at that, John Lambkin quickly walked out of the President's office.

After Lambkin left, Jack intercomed his secretary to get Senator Hanson on the telephone.

"Hanson, Lambkin was just in here and had a note about the Green paper and the account. What in the world did you do?"

Bob Hanson, a wily, robust man with beady eyes and a high-pitched voice nervously replied to the President's obviously demanding question. "I know, I know, I really messed up! I put the wrong Bill in the envelope I sent to the Vice President and sent you the Bill on Farm Subsidies. He should have gotten that one instead. What do you want to do?"

"First of all, Hanson, if this gets out, you are a dead man, you understand? John Lambkin is a fool, but he isn't stupid. He knows when something is out of place or not. I told him that it was probably a new clerk making a reminder note. He didn't swallow it! He left here offended by me and probably has it in mind to investigate this thing. I will take care of him, but I want you to get that little clerk you spend so much time with to lie for you. Tell her to go to the Vice President's office and ask about a note that was attached to Senate Bill 6116. Tell her to tell him that it was a note to remind her to use green routing paper after the Bill is signed!"

"But Mr. President" whined Hanson, "I have never seen a green routing paper after Bill signings!"

"I don't care, you fool, just do it, or something like that; you got it? If this gets out and this thing falls through, we are mud!"

"Yes sir, I will take care of it right away!" wheezed Hanson.

----------- * -----------

"That liar!" fumed John Lambkin as he entered his office. "He's lying and I know it. That mouth of his is going to be rearranged someday!" As he reached for his phone, he noticed that it was four thirty, the time he could catch the one person who could help him catch Jack Prinston in his lies. On the other end of the telephone he heard, "What? I'm busy, this better be good!"

The Vice President knew the voice and the character behind it, that he played poker every

Thursday at four thirty, at the same place. He also knew that the voice was connected to one of the sharpest sleuths around.

"This is John Lambkin, and I have a job for you!" He told him the situation about the "Green Paper" and how he felt. "I want you to find out everything you can about this whole thing. There is more to this than some clerk and a reminder note. Jack Prinston is up to something dirty, and the people will be the losers for it. I want you to give me the ammunition to stop his mouth."

The poker player responded with, "I understand," and hung up the phone.

*

Albert Frank sat with a cup of coffee in one hand and the other waving like he was conducting a flow of traffic. "Deloris, I believe the timing for us to go on that tour of the White House was of God. I believe we were at the right place at the right time. God has something in store for me there! I sure am going to be sensitive to what He is directing there!"

Deloris sat across from Albert, agreeing to his surmising and looking rather canary like.

"Deloris, you look like you know something I don't. What is it?"

"Well, dear, I just remembered how you once told me that you would like to be like Smith Wigglesworth, the famous plumber evangelist. Now here you are going into the White House, being around the leader of the free world and possible being in a position to tell him about Jesus. Isn't that interesting?"

"Yes, sweetheart, it is, but I probably won't see him again. It's not like we will be working together, you know?"

"We will see, Mr. Wiggles!" said Deloris, with a lovely, impish smile.

*

Senator Hanson walked out of the Capital, across the street and to the nearest pay phone. He wanted to make sure that no one would know who he was calling and why, just in case his office phone was tapped.

"Greeley, this is Hanson. Have you made the arrangements with your cousin?"

"Yah! It was arranged two days ago. He said that getting the full sheets after inspection would be no problem. He even arranged for them to be put into a separate trash dumpster, which no one ever checks."

If someone would have been watching Senator Hanson they would have seen him smile and do a little jig at this news. Everything was falling into place for big money for all those involved with this little "Green Paper" diversion.

"OK, Greeley, make sure you let me know when I can start to collect the goods!"

"Got yah, S.H.!"

*

Rebecca ran past Jane Dean and into her father's office.

"Daddy, may I talk with you, please?" Jane arrived just as Rebecca made the request.

"I'm sorry, sir; she was just too fast for me!"

"That's OK, Jane, I will talk with Rebecca!"

"What is it, Becky?" Rebecca looked confused, hurt, and somewhat like a schoolgirl who was all alone on the first day of school.

"Daddy, why doesn't anyone like me?" Jack didn't like intimate conversation and found it hard to speak with his daughter. He really didn't know his daughter, as he was too busy with college, work, and politics when she was growing up. Now that she was an adult he saw her as a flake, weird, and out of touch with reality. Of course, he wasn't going to take time to help her find the reality that would give her peace. He responded, "Honey, people like you, they just don't understand you!"

"But Daddy, people talk about me all the time; I know they do because sometimes I overhear them."

"Well, Becky, if people talk about you behind your back, they are not worth being concerned over. Just go about your life and try to find happiness."

"But, Daddy?" pleaded Rebecca.

"Now, Becky, we have been over these kinds of things before. You just have to go about your life and forget about people who don't like you." Rebecca, having heard this comment before, lowered her head, turned and walked out of her father's office. She felt dejected, rejected, and more confused than before. She walked past Jane Dean's desk and out into the hall, turned the corner and leaned against the wall, just within hearing of Jane's intercom. She heard her father speak to Jane, "Jane, is Rebecca gone?"

"Yes sir, she is!"

"Good, I swear, that girl is crazy as a loon. She sure takes after her mother. They are both nuts!"

Upon hearing this, Rebecca ran up to her room in the family quarters. She was crying uncontrollably, mad, and softly mouthed... "My own daddy doesn't like me. Even he has bad thoughts about me. How could he?"

*

Nora continued to read books on the occult and have "sessions" with Madam Welslie. Thoughts of her husband touching another woman filled her mind. They both had relationships with other people, which was mutually agreed upon, but now after all these years she was jealous. She couldn't stand the thought of Jack touching another woman. This thought possessed her thinking and clouded her judgment. Madam Welslie heard Nora's preoccupation with Jack's hands touching other women, and the rage in her eyes when she puked up the thought. These things even made Welslie a little uneasy.

*

President Prinston's door was open to anyone who had influence and clout. The Oval Office became the trek for anyone who needed a favor and was willing to pad a purse, solidify alliances, or prostrate him or herself to power. The President loved attention, people who were in awe of him and especially lovely women.

The week after the China Room waterfall, Lora Warner, a Lobbyist for "Old Growth Consortium" came to visit the President. Like all the other abasing glad-hander's, Lora wanted favors and the diversion of funds to the Consortium. She was smart, knew how to handle herself and very beautiful. Her being picked by the "Old Growth Consortium" to be their lobbyist was not by mistake. They knew her brain, beauty and bravery in tough situations. They also knew that Lora and Jack had had clandestine meetings when they were in Law School together. Jack had loved Lora deeply, but had to break off the relationship when their college majors changed and she moved to California to attend UCLA. They had never forgotten each other, however.

When Lora was ushered into Jack's office, Jane could see the chemistry between them immediately. Although Jack tried to hide his feelings, his smile, eyes and lips betrayed his heart. Jane knew those outward manifestations of the flesh because many times they were annunciated clearly toward her from Jack.

Lora held out her hand in polite, nervous affirmation of their meeting again. Jack cradled her hand warmly in both of his and kissed her cheek. Still holding her hand he said, "That will be all, Jane, thank you!" As the door closed, Lora and Jack gazed into each other's eyes and fell into each other's arms. It was like they had never been separated. It was the first of many meetings.

The more Jack and Lora met, the more they could not hide their love for each other. Jane knew it, Nora knew it and the staff talked about it. Nora's thoughts were driving her insane, and Jane's were plotting murderous mishaps. Jack had cast the die, and there would be no turning back.

Chapter

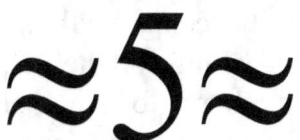

≈5≈

His first week as a plumber's helper was exciting. Albert found being in the White House brought to his occupation the finest tools and equipment money could buy and if it was ever made for plumbing you could get it just by asking. His immediate supervisor was a nice guy, but not too industrious. He would take as much time as he wanted for lunch and simple tasks without the slightest concern over impropriety. Albert, on the other hand, was diligent and believed he was working for God and had to answer to Him first.

Albert's responsibilities took in more than just plumbing, and he was required to repair anything that had to do with metal, pipe, and fixtures. He didn't mind the added work because it made available to him the entire White House and not just plumbing. Many times he would meet, converse with, and give advice to the staff and family. They all saw him as a warm, friendly individual who would always take time with you. It was the latter that introduced him to Nathan Prinston.

It was a warm breezy day; the windows were all open with the curtains flowing in and out. One of those days that slows you down, arrests your attention to creation, and quietly caresses your skin to natures beauty.

Nathan was walking around the White House, looking here and there and not really seeing anything. The spring day had captured his youth and he felt great. There was no need to be in a hurry for the cool air flowing down the corridors seemed to whisper, "Enjoy!" It was in this setting that he would meet his new friend, Albert the plumber.

Albert was kneeling down just outside the Lincoln Bedroom fixing the door handle. He was whistling one of the hymns from church and every now and then would gesture with his hands like the choir director. Nathan stood a short distance off watching the whistling choir director as he orchestrated the door handle into the position that would bring the desired leverage. At the moment the handle adjusted to the desired position, Albert raised his arms and brought them down in punctuated climax like the choir director did at church. With a "ta-da!" he stood to his feet, with the sound of Nathan clapping and shouting "Bravo, bravo!"

"Hi," said Nathan. "My name is Nathan Prinston!"

Albert, with a little bit of embarrassment, replied, "Hi, my name is Albert Frank nice to meet you!"

With a big smile, Nathan declared, "I sure like the way you work. You coaxed that door handle into place with a whistle and a smile."

"Well, I have learned that a soft touch, gentle persuasion and a tune unto the Lord makes things fall into place much easier."

"Hey, man, that sure sounds right!" was Nathan's reply to the wisdom he had just heard. A close friendship developed as Nathan followed Albert around the White House, fixing little items that had been neglected over the last few years.

They would talk about anything and everything. Albert introduced Nathan to chess, and many times they would play in the storage room during lunch and after work. Since Nathan was taking time out from college for a semester, he had the freedom to adjust his schedule to Albert's.

It was during one of their lunchtime chess indulgements that Albert interjected God's love and sovereignty to Nathan. Nathan was completely ignorant of God's love and Jesus' sacrifice on his behalf. Albert told him things that were outside of his sphere of influence; Neither of Nathan's parents, relatives, nor friends had anything to do with God or the concept of God. He was, however, a pliable and moldable heart in the loving and capable hands of the evangelist plumber.

———————— * ————————

Greely contacted his cousin, a skinny balding man with large eyes and a temperament that matched the viciousness of a scared dog on a dark night. This cousin had gotten his job at the Department of Treasury printing plant by direct intervention of Senator Hanson. Hanson's and Greely's families farmed adjacent to each other in Minnesota. Greely owed Hanson many back favors for helping him evade the law during his youth. The Cousin was an unscrupulous individual that would do anything for money, legal or otherwise. Recruiting him was a easy as sticking a piece of meat in front of a dog. He would bite at anything and accept any explanation given him. He just didn't care!

"Hey Cuz', how's it going?"

"Pretty good man, how about you?"

"Very well, very well; are we all set for the first delivery for the Green Paper?"

"Yep, you can pick it up tonight, after eleven!"

"Just outside the gate then, where we planned?"

"Yes sir, but don't use a flashlight or have your lights on your car. Just pull up to the fence with your lights off; walk to the gate and give it a gentle push. It will open easily. The paper will be in a white duffle bag."

"OK, Cuz I got yah! Have there been any problems getting the paper to the trash container?"

"No, I made sure that the camera going to that area is out of order for a while. It will be out of order every time we need to make a drop!" Hanson was pleased and just a little bit nervous, as tonight he would pick up the paper. "See you later, Cuz', I will settle up with you at the usual! Good by!"

*

Wannetta Morales was still shook up after being accosted by Rebecca on the stairs. She had never experienced anything like it in all the time she had been in America.

She originally came from Mexico City twenty years ago, and after becoming a citizen of the U.S.A. she applied for the maid's job at the White House.

Getting the job was luck because there were many applicants, but most never fit the requirements for the job. She, however, had education, a clean police record, and was trained for the position by working in Mexico City at the Mexico Hyatt Hotel, which only catered to dignitaries from around the world.

She was short, athletic, and very responsive to her environment.

The evening after the attack by Rebecca, Wannetta knelt with her husband praying for the lost daughter of the president. Their cries on behalf of the most important family in the country could be heard up the stairs and in the ears of their children. They prayed in English, as was their custom since moving to the U.S., for the sake of the children. "Oh God, we beseech you on behalf of the Prinstons. Father, help them to know you. Bring life into that home, their souls, and their understanding. May they come to you through Jesus! Father, help Rebecca to be free of the demons that posses her and her mother. May she realize the dangers of the occult. In Jesus name, Amen!" When they were finished, their children came downstairs and joined them

"Momma, why do you pray for those people who treat you so badly?" the littlest one asked.

"Well, Meha, they are lost souls that will go to hell if they don't come to Jesus. They need help and just don't know it. Our prayers can open the doors for that help to get to them!"

"I see, Momma. Then I will pray for them too when I go to bed!" Such were the likes of the personalities around Rebecca and her family. She would have no excuse for denying eternity.

*

The next day around 4 PM, just before quitting time, when people are busy getting ready to depart work and are not to aware of happenings around them, a lone figure was bringing the printing press of the 100 dollar bill sheets too a halt at the Treasury Printers.

The 100 dollar bills, which were called "Yellows" now by the population, because of their color, were an artist's delight. The color had been changed in 2020 because of rampant forgery and was multi colored with the distinct background of yellow. You could see one from across the room.

Many of the other U.S. bills had been color changed as well with artistic and anti-counterfeiting elements added. The $1 dollar was reddish, the $5 was still green, the $10 was bluish, the $20 a light tan, the $50 had a blackish tint and, of course, the $100 was yellowish.

The one hundred dollar bills, which were printed on sheets of fifty, were meticulously watched through the whole process. However, there is a time when someone, if they were unscrupulous, could manage to confiscate a few sheets on the way to the inspection room. The inspection room was the place where every fiftieth sheet was taken to be examined for flaws. They get to the room by being put on a cart at the end of the day, which by then contains around two hundred. On this particular day however, there were about three hundred. The "Cuz'" put the extra 100 there.

He took the cart as usual, went down the work hall and toward the inspection room. As he turned the corner, where the usual security camera was observing, he walked over to the special trashcan that he had put there earlier and deposited 100 sheets of fifty 100-dollar bills. He would do this every week for one year, without being caught. This taking of $500,000.00 a week would never be missed because of the quantity that was being produced and the counter being wrongly set each day by the "Cuz." In the year that our greedy group of political good fellows stuck their hand in the nation's cookie jar, they stole twenty six million dollars, and no one was the wiser. Senator Hanson, Greely and his cousin each got ten percent each and President Jack Prinston pigeonholed the rest.

*

"May I speak to Vice President Lambkin please?"
"Whom may I say is calling?" asked the secretary.
"This is Mr. Green!"
"I'm sorry, sir, I don't have you on his list of call-ins!"
"Just tell him. He will speak to me, just try!"

"I will try sir!" said the suspicious secretary, but complied, as the caller seemed to know that the Vice President would take his call.

"Mr. Vice President, there is a Mr. Green on the telephone for you and would like to speak with you!"

"Oh, yes, I will, sure, what line?"

"It's line two, sir!"

John Lambkin was frustrated and nervous as he picked up the phone. "What in the world are you doing calling me on this line. I thought we agreed that I would call you?"

"Yah, yah, I know but you haven't called in awhile so I figured I'd better check in. Our friend has had a lot of contact with Senator Hanson, who has been making a lot of phone calls outside of the capital using the pay phone across the street. It looks like he is trying to hide something. I have my friends on the phone line with that booth. I will keep you posted, sir!"

"OK, Mr. Green, but don't call me here again. I will call you, period! Good by!" The VP knew that he was on to something and he was determined to catch the President in lies and skullduggery.

*

Senator Hanson, after getting the news from Greely that the "Green Paper" would be ready for pick up that night, made arrangements with the President for distribution. The President would have Secret Agent J.B. Whitaker pick up a box at Senator Hanson's home. Agent Whitaker would not know that the box contained the ill-gotten gain from Greely, the Cuz or

Hanson. He was told that it contained two bottles of champagne that Senator Hanson gave to the President every week. They even put two bottles in the box for sound purposes. Agent Whitaker never found out that he carried his tax money directly to his President.

The Bureau of Engraving and Printing was lit up as usual, which made Hanson very nervous. He had passed that building everyday without any fear or concern, but with the building lit up this night, and what he was about to do un-nerved him. Those lights seemed to explode with the illuminating war cry of injustice at the highest level. Greely's Cuz was right; you didn't need any lights as you pulled up to the gate. The gate was well lit and no area of the dumpster/trash area was without luminescence. The Senator could not figure out why he was told not to bring a flashlight. He soon found out as he pushed on the gate. With a gentle push on the gate, it opened and the lights went out. It was pitch black. Good ole Cuz had it fixed to have the lights go out when the gate was open those nights. He ran to the area of the "special" trash container and reached in. His hands felt the duffle bag and he yanked. Out it came easily, but the lid made a loud "bang!" as it hit the ground. He excitedly grabbed it and returned it to its place and then scurried back to his car. As the gate closed gently, the lights went back on. "This is not as heavy as I thought $500,000.00 would be!" he thought to himself, as he drove away. He slithered his way home, down to his basement and distributed the "goods" into different boxes for himself and his fellow dealers of dirty money. The first of the twenty six million was now in the hands of the so-called elite of our country.

———————— * ————————

It was midnight and Agent Whitaker had just returned from Senator Hanson's home with the box of "champagne." He rang the President's quarters and told him that he had picked up the box from Senator Hanson's home. The President told him to bring it up. After receiving the box, the President told the Agent to meet him in the kitchen. "I suppose you were wondering what was in that box, Agent Whitaker?"

"No, sir, I didn't give it a thought. Anything special I should know about though?"

"Well, Mr. Whitaker, it is the finest champagne money can buy. Would'ya like a glass?"

"Well, sir, I'm on duty, you know!"

"Agent Whitaker, your boss has just given you an order to drink, so drink you must!" The unsuspecting agent shrugged his shoulder, grabbed the glass and said, "Who am I to argue with the boss of the U. S. of A!" The President told the agent that it was a weekly promise made to him by Senator Hanson for the President's help on getting him into office. He promised to give him two bottles of champagne every week. "I made him promise to have it delivered every midnight to make it more interesting. Just one of those little games we guys play, you know!"

Chapter

≈6≈

The first four years of President Prinston's administration went without a glitch. Yes, there was the usual political party bickering, but as a whole, everything went very well. Since industry had a handle on research and devoted much of its profits on anything that would correct the nation's sicknesses, everyone was a winner. Even though much of corporate earnings went to research, there were still millions and even billions being made by the shareholders. No one complained.

Technology had advanced so fast that the Internet of the late 90's looked like a play toy. To communicate with anyone in the universe the UWW, the Universal Wide Web had been established. Since man had gone back to the moon and just recently colonized Mars, there was the need for instant communication in the universe. The UWW could send and receive email, voice, and video into any room connected with a small handheld device the size of the old CD disks.

Human cloning research was just at the trial stage and there were many people signed up to be the first. Where this area of man's search to become a creator would end, no one knew. Cloning was scary to many, but yet intriguing to most. Even those who were against man's attempt to be God wanted to see what sort of freak would be the results of these dabbling's of flesh and nature.

Jack Prinston had his hand in every aspect of research and social engineering. Now that he was in his second term of office and giving the nation what they wanted, everyone who didn't know him personally loved him. He was the most popular president ever.

You would have thought with his popularity, "Green Money" stealing, and the recent relationship renewal with Lora Warner, that he would be happy. But just the opposite was going on in his soul; he was miserable. None of the material or emotional things of the flesh seemed to bring him joy. When he did feel good, there always seemed to be a shadow of foreboding reality, like something was lost and could never be restored. He would wake up during the night with this sense that someone was calling his name, gently but firmly demanding a change. Try as he may to drown his miserable feelings, he couldn't. There were times he did sense some relief, and they were when he was with his son.

*

Nathan and Albert by now were friends. Nathan would spend as much time with him as possible. He would listen to the evangelist plumber with rapt attention and awed admiration.

It was cold outside and the boiler room was the place to be for Nathan, as he watched Albert fix a broken faucet handle. Albert was his usual self, confident of his position and sure of his mission for God. He understood that his life was not his own, and that there was more to his life than fixing faucets for the President of the United States. Every place and every moment were to be dedicated to his Lord. Today was no different!

Just last night as he and Delores had prayed they had this strong sense that God was dealing with Nathan Prinston. Their prayers on behalf of the President seemed to shift from him to his son. Although they felt that Nathan was closer to God then he realized, they felt that Jack Prinston had a long way to go. However, their prayers of open request moved from the passive style that many use in seeking God, to an intercession of their souls. It seemed as if they were caught in this whirlwind of spiritual warfare of Godly wonderment.

"God, we beseech you to bring Nathan Prinston to yourself. Direct his steps to the light of your truth. May he see clearly the cross, his sin, and your forgiveness! Help him to hear with new ears, see with new eyes, and comprehend with a new understanding! In Jesus name, Amen!"

Delores and Albert cried, laughed and excitedly moved around the room like they had just won a million dollars. In their hearts, "their knower," they knew God heard and would answer.

But this day Nathan started the conversation. "Albert, how did you become a plumber?"

"Well, my boy, I kind of fell into it by mistake. I wanted to be a surgeon from the time I was a young boy. I could just see myself cutting open the human body, repairing the diseased or broken parts, and making the person better."

"Why didn't you go to college for it?"

"I did go to college for it, but I got sidetracked! To make money during college I went to work with my uncle who was a plumber. He had his own business and needed help during the summer. I worked for him two summers and just before going back to college at the end of the second year I realized what I really enjoyed in life and it was plumbing. Go figure, from doctor to plumber!" Albert looked at Nathan for the usual you must be crazy for becoming a plumber instead of a doctor look. But what he saw was acceptance, understanding and a look that said, "Why not?"

Albert continued, "I prayed about…" but couldn't finish the sentence as Nathan interrupted.

"What do you mean you prayed about it? Why didn't you just make your mind up and do it?"

"Well, Nathan, I am a Christian. I love God with my whole being, and I believe that we should get our heavenly Father's approval for everything we do!"

Nathan looked away with sadness in his face. "What is it, Nathan?" said Albert. "Why do you look so hurt?"

Nathan, making sure his face was now completely in the opposite direction replied, "When you said getting your father's approval, it made me think of my own dad and getting his approval. He could care less what I or Rebecca would do!" Albert's heart went out to Nathan. Although Nathan didn't understand what Albert had just said, Albert could see the hurt and rejection in the President's son.

"Nathan, I'm so sorry to see your hurt, but I was talking about God, not my natural father. May I help you with your pain of rejection?"

"I'm not rejected!" replied Nathan with the shy smile of hurt upon his lips.

"Yes, I understand, Nathan, but you know, there is 'One' who never rejects us nor turns away from us. He cares about everything you do and say. He loves you beyond measure, takes care of you even when you don't know it, and is always willing to listen."

Nathan looked up, turned to Albert and said, "I know you are talking about God! But why would God care about me? I have never had anything to do with him nor even believed he was real! Why would he love me?"

By now Albert had moved closer to Nathan and had put his arm around the confused young man. "Nathan, He cares for you because He made you. He loves you because you are made in His image. He wants you to know Him so that you can have fellowship and life with Him."

Nathan buried his shoulder into Albert's armpit and put his arm around Albert's waist.

"My friend, would you like to know God who made you?"

"What must I do?" sheepishly asked Nathan.

"Buddy, do you believe you are a sinner and need help?"

"If you mean do I do bad things and have not even sought after God, yes!"

"I want you to know, Nathan." Albert continued. "That God became a man, like you and me…His name was Jesus. He took the punishment for all mankind's sins. Someone had to die for all the bad and rebellion against God. There was no human capable of doing this because every human had sin. Therefore, God became a man and died himself in the flesh for every person's sins. All you have to do is believe that fact, the fact that God really did that for you. That you are a sinner in need of help, and only God can give you that help. Do you believe that, Nathan?"

Nathan looked Albert directly in the eyes, with tears in his, and said, "Yes!"

"Would you mind kneeling with me and talking to God in prayer?" Albert quietly asked with joy in his heart and tears in his eyes, gently tugging on Nathan's hand.

"No, sir, I wouldn't mind!"

After they were on their knees, Albert was about to guide Nathan in a prayer when he heard him say, "God, I am sorry for not seeking you out years ago. I have ignored you my whole life. I am sorry for taking you for granted and for my many sins. Please forgive me for my rotten life and the ways I have lived. If you died for my sins I receive your forgiveness now. Also, God, thank you for becoming a man like me, and taking my punishment. Jesus, I want to serve you and live for you from now on. Amen!" That was that, there was no guiding, no repeating or "follow after me." Nathan had made his peace with God.

*

Wannetta Morales was cleaning the Blue Room when she felt this urge to pray for Albert the plumber. She snuck into the nearest bathroom and sat in one of the stalls and prayed for about ten minutes for Albert Frank the plumber. She felt that something was taking place that would change the lives of many. She was correct!

*

Delores Frank was in the kitchen washing the lunchtime dishes when she had this overpowering vision in her mind's eye of a young man falling into the arms of a gentle man. She had learned years ago to never let those types of leadings go without prayer. Although she didn't know the circumstance in this situation, she knew enough about spiritual warfare to intercede for whomever the Lord was dealing with. She stopped the washing, got down on her knees and prayed. She prayed for the soul with whom God was dealing, and then she prayed for her husband.

*

Nathan looked up after his prayer. You could see tears of joy and the quivering smile of a new son of God, just released from the clutches of sin. Albert stood, danced, and hugged his new brother in the Lord.

"Praise God, thank you, Jesus!! Wow, that is why I am here in the White House! Yes!" he exclaimed as Nathan looked on. "Nathan, you are one of God's children now. You are in the family of God and the kingdom of God. God is your eternal Father, your provider, and protector. You are His!"

"Now, if only my earthly father knew Him like I do!" said Nathan.

Albert explained to Nathan that the best way for his dad to come to Jesus would be through their prayers. Since his dad was the man he was, he probably wouldn't listen to any preaching. It would be best to pray, live a godly life, and use the opportunities that God gave them.

"I think you are right, Albert. Let's pray for Dad right now." was Nathan's reply. They prayed for Jack Prinston and his openness to the gospel of love, repentance and forgiveness.

*

The rest of the day for Wannetta Morales seemed to be anticlimactic. The time of prayer in the bathroom grotto seemed to say, your work for today has been finished. As she went about the remainder of her duties she was in contact with her Lord by means of inner peace and praying in the spirit. Things like the ten minutes of prayer in the bathroom had taken place before, but for some reason she felt that this time was special. As she turned the corner to the kitchen, she saw Albert the plumber and wanted to ask him what he had been doing about an hour ago.

"Hello, Señor Frank, may I speak with you, please?"

"Sure, what can I do for you?"

"I hope you don't think I am too forward, but I must ask you about something that happened about an hour ago. Where you doing anything special about that time?"

"Why, what do you mean?" came back Albert's guarded reply. You see he didn't want to be fired for "preaching" while on duty.

"Mr. Frank, I am a Christian and love Jesus. About an hour ago I had the urge to pray for you; was something going on that you needed help with?"

Albert was thrown off a little bit by her straight forward and honest approach, but admired her for it. "Well, bless your heart, sister, I too am a Christian and, yes, I was doing something very important for the kingdom of God about an hour ago!"

Wannetta smiled, raised her arms in praise and shouted, "Praise the Lord!"

Albert told her to calm down, as not everyone in the "House" liked that sort of thing.

"Yes, yes, you are right, I need to control myself. But, what was it you were doing?" Wannetta giggling asked. He told her and they both rejoiced, but quietly. They made a pact to pray for each other and the Prinston family.

———————— * ————————

The next day at breakfast, Nathan sat eating his food with more enjoyment than he had for years. Jack,

Nora and Rebecca sat eating with their usual quiet demeanor.

"Well, how you all doing?" broke the silence from the new man of faith. "What are y'all's plans for today?" Nathan queried. "Anything special?"

Rebecca looked over at her smiling faced brother and replied, "What do you care, smiley?"

"I care sis, I care, just wanted to know what's up?"

"Nothing!" came her reply.

"How about you Mom, anything special today?" Not waiting for a reply, Nathan asked again, "How about you Dad, anything special?"

Jack, not answering the question asked, "What's gotten into you, why all the questions?"

"I don't know, I just love you all and I am interested in your lives!" Nathan responded.

"Right," said Rebecca as she left the room.

"That's sweet, son!" said Nora as she moved to the sink.

"Well, son it's running the country as usual for me, thanks for asking!" came Jack's reply. However, as he replied, there was this feeling of acceptance from his son that he never felt before, or at least hadn't noticed before, although it was always there for the taking.

"Hey, buddy, I don't have a lot of time today, but how about us getting together for a swim soon?"

"Great Dad, it's a date, just let me know when, OK?

Chapter

Twelve months had passed since the poker player, or "Mr. Green," as he called himself whenever he talked to John Lambkin, had begun his investigation into Senator Hanson's weekly dark foraging's outside the Bureau of Engraving and Printing. Green kept notes on Hanson's daily activities and his every move, whether alone or with family. Hanson had no idea that his life was being watched or that Mr. Green knew his schedule better than he did himself. Mr. Green had contacts with people who were close to the Senator and his secretary, who enjoyed the ten and twenty dollars she would receive for information on Hanson's schedule.

Getting the money each week from the trash can at the Bureau of Engraving and Printing was very easy for Hanson. Although he always felt scared, there was just enough excitement in it to keep him cautious. He never suspected that he was being watched except for the one time he thought he saw someone follow him home from a typical night's scavenging.

On that particular night, he drove around the Bureau of Engraving and Printing building three times before departing on his usual route. He passed Mr. Green, who was sitting in his car pretending to be a drunk sleeping it off. Mr. Green, obviously was not intoxicated, but followed the thief home and surreptitiously made his way to his basement window and watched the unloading of the duffle bag. Poker Player could only see portions of a table and the bag, but he could clearly see the box and champagne bottles. It was the box that he would keep his eyes on for the next few months. He noticed that every week Hanson went through the same routine at the Bureau of Engraving and Printing, the duffle bag being emptied, and the box and bottles of champagne being taken out by Secret Agent Whitaker. He followed the box!

*

Rebecca by now had become totally lost from reality and was visibly under a power not of herself. No one knew the direct effect that Nora's occult practices had on her daughter, but it was deeply and insanely possessive.

Nora thought she was doing right when she consulted mediums when she was pregnant with Rebecca. Wanting a healthy child and desiring that child to be "protected" from evil, Nora was lured to unknown forces that she thought were good. What she did instead was open the door for her child to be first harassed and then possessed by demons. Rebecca was now living in a foggy world of hate, suspicion and death. The more she thought about those who disliked her the more she plotted revenge.

Rebecca was beyond hope, and on more than one occasion, she overheard her father planning her committal to an institution for the insane. He would not make the final arrangements for her being secreted away until after he was out of office, however, because his reputation was more important to him than his daughter's well being.

*

Realizing the importance of his investigative snooping, our Poker Player decided that he had better contact someone other than the Vice President about his observations of Senator Hanson. He contacted the FBI on February 1st.

*

Jack Prinston and Lora Warner were now an item, at least in private. Jack found ways to have clandestine meetings with Lora and tried to keep her from the White House as much as possible. There were times, however, that she would have to come to meetings along with other lobbyists who explained their client's positions on bills that the President was trying to push through Congress. Whenever Lora would be at those meetings, Jack made sure she could hang around afterwards.

After one of the Lobbyist meetings, Lora was with Jack near the coffee cubbyhole. They were just talking and nothing else, but Nora and Jane Dean found them at the same time. Nora was coming from one direction and Jane from another. Although they were innocent this time, both Jack and Lora looked nervously guilty and didn't know what to say. Nora acted like it was no big deal, but was seething inside while Jane pretended to just want coffee. While getting the coffee, however, she managed to splash a little on Lora's dress. "Oh, I'm sorry!" she murmured as she and walked away. Jack's wife and personal secretary were, at least in their eyes, has-beens. Jack knew it, Lora knew it, and worst of all, the two former love objects knew it. Nora washed her hands over and over after touching Jack because he had been with Lora. Her thinking became so clouded that she thought she was vicariously washing Lora's contamination from Jack's hands. Jane found a quiet place and sobbed her heart out, not really believing that Jack had given his heart to someone else.

*

After Poker Player notified the FBI, he continued to observe Senator Hanson. With the guidance of an FBI agent who went with him on the weekly stake-outs at the Bureau of Engraving and Printing, Poker Player was now a part of an official "Bureau" investigation. He was told to keep Vice President Lambkin informed and not leave out any details of the operation except that the FBI was also involved. The FBI believed that the V.P. was not involved in any of the crooked dealings, but did not want to lose information just in case he was. Poker Player was not breaking the law and for that reason saved himself from future adverse scrutiny.

———————— * ————————

Although the President was managing to keep his life in an orderly fashion, his spirit was in chaos. Lora fed the outer man but could not touch his soul with relief. He found himself digging deeper into schemes that would flood his secret strong boxes and Swiss accounts, but not pour one ounce of personal satisfaction of good into his spirit. He was ready for the light!

———————— * ————————

Nathan had been walking in his new life for awhile now. His knowledge of scripture was on par with Albert's and maybe a little beyond that. He was an apt student of God's word and devoured it like a starving castaway who had just been found. He was ready for any challenge and was wise with his time and very sensitive to God's leading. He wanted to talk to his parents about God's love and forgiveness, but felt that God was saying "Wait, there will be the right time!" He was patient, wise with his words, and willing. Meanwhile nothing escaped his keen sense of observation or his sensitivity to the Holy Spirit.

On one particular day Jack needed a break from his hectic schedule so he called the family quarters to talk to Nathan.

"Hey, son, what you up to? Want to go for a swim?"

Nathan, who was always ready to spend time with his dad, most aggressively replied, "Yes sir! When?"

"Right now in the pool. I'll meet you there."

Nathan missed the phone hook as he slipped out of the chair and tried to cradle the handset into place. He was excited and willing to spend time with his dad, but felt like he was on the verge of some spiritual adventure that would wet their lives more than the water of the White House pool. He was right!

Jack met Nathan at the pool dressed in his conservative trunks with the Seal of the President of the United States embroidered upon it. Nathan came running down the stairs wearing a baggy pair of old blue jeans cut off and tattered. He had a smile on his face that said "Fun!"

As he hit the bottom step just a few feet from his father, he threw down his towel and lunged at his dad pulling him into the water. Down they went, with Nathan holding Jack's head under water. As they came up, Jack was spitting and smiling like he had just found a valve in his person that released a years worth of tension. More was done in that one dunking with his son then many sessions with people who wanted something from him. He was open for input from his son.

"Dad, this is great. We haven't done this for a long time! Why did we wait?"

Jack by now was totally at rest and seemingly without a care. He responded, "Son, I'm not sure, but I think I lost sight of the important things in life. Being the President was the most important thing in my life, before I got it. Now, after five years, it doesn't have the glitter or the pull on me like it had. I find myself doing things for power and glory, but without realizing that I am just going through motions without my heart being in it." He caught himself, *"Was this Jack Prinston, opening up and being intimate with his son?"* He surmised, *"Maybe it's because Nathan is a young adult now, and I can be personal with him."* Whatever it was Jack liked it. He went on.

"Nathan, you sure seemed to have changed. What has gotten into you?" Jack was floating on his back, sucking in water and then spouting out like a tugboat. By now, Nathan was totally immersed into this moment with his dad. He was at peace, very much aware of God's presence and ready for anything. But his Dad's question took him off guard. *What should he say or d? Should he skim over the question and find something else to talk about? What, what should he do?* Just then he heard a familiar inner voice that he had become accustomed to. It was the voice of the Spirit and he said, *"Remember, I told you to wait for the proper time; it is now!"*

Nathan swam over to his father, cupped his hands into a scoop and squirted him in the face, saying, "Dad, I have found peace with and in God!" He settled down, resting his feet on the bottom and waited for Jack's reply. Jack didn't move, other than to wipe his face after the squirt. He then slowly rolled over, face under water, and thought. Motionless, Nathan waited for some reaction from his dad.

When Jack came up for air, he said, "Tell me about it!"

Inside Nathan there were fireworks, ice cream, cool breezy days, gentle loving hands, and words of acceptance all at one time making his endorphins flow and causing him to be in a state of euphoria. God had told him to wait for the right time and now here it was. He was going to make the best of it.

"Dad, do you know Albert Frank, the plumber?"

"Why, yes, I met him the day the water pipes broke near the China Room. He's a great guy."

"Well Dad, he is a Christian. He told me about God's love, forgiveness and acceptance."

Jack didn't move and by now had stopped dead in the water with his feet on the bottom. He was looking straight at Nathan, with the accepting look of love for his son, slowly moving his hands back and forth to keep himself steady in the water. His eyes projected the cry within his heart that whispered, "Tell me more!"

"Dad, Albert told me that God loves us and wants us to know Him, personally. He told me that God became a man in order to take the punishment for our rebellion and sins toward Him."

Jack remained still, as he stated, "I guess I have always believed there was a God, but I tried to ignore him or pretend he never existed. If there is a God, then I am in trouble!"

Nathan's heart went out to his dad as he replied, "Well, Dad, there is a God and I think you are in trouble! But, you know, you can be made right with Him!"

"How is that, son?"

"Well, dad, do you believe you are a sinner? That you have been living for yourself and not God?"

"Son, I do believe there is sin! I do believe there is right and wrong! I do believe there is a God because somebody or something had to make the universe, it didn't make itself. Yes, I do believe I have sinned and have been living for myself!"

Nathan put his hand on his dad's shoulder. "Dad, Jesus who was God in flesh, took your sins and punishment so that you could be free from them and know Him! All you have to do to be free, Dad, is repent of your sins and turn your life over to God!"

Before Nathan could continue, the White House Butler entered the poolroom and cleared his throat to get the President's attention.

"Excuse me, sir, Senator Hanson is on the telephone and insists on speaking to you!"

"Fredrick, can't he wait?"

"I don't think so, sir, he did insist that I interrupt you!"

"All right Fredrick, I'll take it in the side room. Thank you."

"I'm sorry, Nathan, but I guess I'd better take that call," said Jack, with a perturbed look upon his face. "I'll be right back."

Nathan couldn't believe his ears; just when he was getting somewhere with his dad, they were interrupted. He knew who the cause of this interruption was; it was the enemy of all men's souls! He began to pray and stayed in an attitude of prayer until Jack returned.

*

"Hello, Hanson, you better have a good reason for calling me now! What is it?" Jack was in no mood for Hanson's paranoia

"Jack, I think someone has been watching me pick up the Green Paper each week!"

"I hope you are just being paranoid. Who do you think it is?" quietly asked Jack.

"I don't know, but on more than one occasion, I thought I saw someone in my yard and close to my basement window, and only on the nights of the pick up!"

"Well, Hanson, I think we had better stop our little five finger discount. We have made more than enough anyway. Tell Greely to close down the operation. Tonight! Do you understand?"

"Yes sir, I understand. Good-bye!" wheezed Hanson.

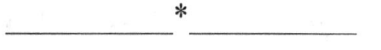

Nathan was waiting for his father and knew that something was up when he returned and picked up his towel.

"I'm sorry, son, but there are things I must take care of. We'll have to continue our conversation later. I promise we'll do this again!" At that Jack turned and walked up the stairs, leaving a very disappointed ambassador of the cross.

Hanson contacted Greely and told him to stop the Green Paper operation.

"Greely, stop all Green Paper operations. Don't take one sheet more, or you'll be on your own without protection. You understand?"

"Yes, I understand. We have more than enough anyway. What should I tell my cousin?"

"Tell him to quit his job and leave town or better yet, the country. He has more than enough for the rest of his life. But just make sure he is not around this area anymore!"

"Got yah, S.H.. What should I do?" knowingly asked Greely. Hanson didn't like Greely but only used him for special deals and really didn't care what he did, but he knew it would be best for him to get lost also.

"Get lost yourself!"

Greely read between the lines and knew enough of these sorts of things and that it would be best for his longevity to leave town as well.

"I understand, S.H. I'm gone! See yah!"

*

Jack didn't trust Hanson's willpower or stamina of silence and decided he better take care of this loose end. It didn't matter to him that he had made $18,200,000.00 off Hanson's contacts and midnight trips over this last year. All he cared about was not getting caught and living his life the way he liked, even though that was almost unbearable lately. He made arrangements.

*

"Hurry, he'll be coming around the bend in just a few minutes! We've got to get that tanker across the road now! Move it, move it!" yelled one of the men hiding in the shadows.

This particular bend in the road was dark, curvy and dangerous. It was the perfect place to waylay an unsuspecting Senator. These two deadly characters of murderous mayhem moved quickly with the precision of trained commandos. They knew their dark art of mayhem and seemed to maneuver the gas tanker like they had done this sort of thing before. Driving it forward and then backing it up with one quick sharp turn put the vehicle into the most dangerous position for the desired effect; death! The tall, lanky driver set the parking brake, opened the door and jumped out of the stolen tanker, just as the other, short, perpetrator opened the emptying valve and let the gas flow onto the ground and all around. This whole operation took only about a minute before they were off to hide in the woods to observe and insure that the deed would be done right.

Around the bend Senator Hanson came, driving his usual racetrack speed on this particular road to his daughter's house in the woods. He imagined himself as one of those top-notch drivers at the Indy 500, with driving gloves on and the window open. It didn't matter to him that at night this road could be a killer. He only wanted to feel the speed. Just at the last bend, on the tightest spot in the road he saw it; a gas tanker in his path. He couldn't stop and he didn't have room to maneuver past. At 67 miles an hour he hit the tanker just at the valve spewing area. He didn't have a chance, as the sparks from the collision and impact-crumbling car made for one large torch.

Poker Player's tailing sedan was too far behind to be of any assistance to the speedster Senator. Senator Robert Hanson was dead! The slithering murderers ran off into the woods and out of sight.

F.B.I. and local officials did an extensive investigation of the Hanson/Tanker incident and concluded that it was an accidental homicide. The tanker had been reported stolen earlier in the evening. The best guess was that the thieves did not know those hills and tried to turn the tanker around at the tightest and most dangerous area on the road. They were never caught.

The nation mourned and President Prinston eulogized him with flowery words and praise befitting a Senator.

Since Senator Hanson was dead and there was no other person involved with the midnight trash can incidents, the F.B.I. let their investigation of the Senator rest, but it was not closed. They told Poker Player that there were no reports of wrongdoing at the Bureau of Engraving and Printing and that they had suspended the investigation; his services were no longer needed.

Secret Agent J.B. Whitaker was questioned about the midnight deliveries made to the President's quarters each week from Senator Hanson, but the agent believed in the champagne story and everything was dropped. Only time would tell if the true story would be told.

71

Chapter

T he news of Senator Hanson's death made the Vice President livid. He had thought he would have evidence enough to accuse and then find the President guilty of underhanded dealings. But with Hanson dead, the V.P. could not put pressure on anyone to finger the lying mouth of his nemesis now. Poker Player told him that he suspected foul play, but could not prove anything. Thievery was common in D.C. and just might have been what it looked like, a tanker theft that had gone bad. He had a gut instinct that it was no accident, however, because he had tried the gate at the Bureau of Engraving and Printing the night before, and it wouldn't open, Hanson had not shown up that night either. This was too coincidental for him! After a few telephone calls and a little shoe work he found that one employee had just quit and could not be found. He knew his name, where he lived, and what his job was at the Bureau of Engraving and Printing; it had to do with the sheets of one hundred dollar bills. This all was good theory but not evidence. He had to back off for now.

John Lambkin seethed with the thought of not getting something on Prinston. The way Jack spoke at the funeral for Senator Hanson made him more suspicious than ever. But the weekly midnight deliveries from the Hansons to the President were just too much to accept. He knew the President was lying and he wanted to shut that lying mouth once and for all, but how?

*

"Good morning, Washington Herald Newspaper, may I help you?"

"Yes, I would like to speak to Susan Collins, please."

"Whom may I say is calling?"

"Just tell her I may have the biggest story of her career!"

"But, whom may I say is calling?"

"Never mind that. Just get her OK?"

"Yes sir!" The receptionist at the Herald was used to calls like that and tried to keep them from getting to the overworked reporters because they usually were crazy cranks complaining about an article. She decided to let this call through, however. It was the best thing she ever did.

"This is Susan Collins, may I help you?"

"Yah, how would you like some very interesting dirt on the late Senator Hanson?" Poker Player knew his value to the V.P. had come to an end and wanted another source of income. Even if it wouldn't be much, he would take anything he could get. Miss Collins was a sharp reporter, in her late twenties with ten years experience. She had a reputation for being fair, smart, and courageous, and many a time she had gotten the scoop when others had no idea there was even a story.

"What do you mean dirt on Senator Hanson? Who is this?"

"Not so fast, missy! I want to know if you will talk to me about Hanson?"

"Well, I'm not going to talk to anyone I don't know or won't tell me their name!"

"Now listen, I'll give you the story, but I am not going to give you my name. Anything I give you will be in secret and in the shadows. If you can't handle that, I'll go someplace else!"

"But what if you are some kook who just wants to take advantage of me?"

"Sure, lady, I have thoughts of you! Get serious; I am!"

"Where could we meet?" Susan thought this was crazy, but she had learned from the past that much of the weird brought tons of information.

"O.K., I'll meet you at that little coffee shop on fifth and thirteenth. I think it's called 'The Dark Roast,' whispered Poker Player.

"Now wait a minute, I thought you said our meetings would be in secret? A coffee shop doesn't sound too secret!" demanded Miss Collins.

"Hey, don't second guess me, little girl. Just be there at 4 PM tomorrow!"

Susan responded to the little girl remark with a sharp reply and an in your face command. "O.K., I will be there, but don't call me little girl, friend! Good-bye!"

*

Jane buzzed her boss and asked if she could talk to him. Obviously, he wasn't about to say no; after all, she was his secretary. She opened the door to the oval office as she had done many times, for business and pleasure, and each time as she entered the bastion of the most powerful person in the world she was awed. The splendor of power and the importance of the surroundings never became second place to Jane, even though she conducted herself without restraints many times in its environment. This time she felt like an uninvited guest, even though it was her place of business and the link to the man she loved with her whole heart.

Jack sat with his legs up on the desk that J.F.K. had made famous, reading over some papers and drinking from a coffee cup that had the Great Seal on it.

"Sir," said Jane with a little bit of embarrassment. "I want to talk to you about something very personal!"

"Sir?" Why so formal, Jane? Please...Jack!" said her supposed lover. "Come here and sit down!" said Jack motioning to his lap. Jane complied and moved into the place she would rather be than any other in the universe. "Now, what is it sweetheart?"

"Jack, I want to know if you still love me."

"Why, yes, I do, I always have...you are my best friend, my sweetheart and, well you know! Need I say more?" Jack mouthed the words but the feeling and emotions did not match his body language and his look-away eyes.

Jane knew in her heart that Jack was no longer hers but didn't want to believe it. The tension in Jack's body confirmed her fears and made her a little sick to her stomach. She gave him a peck upon the cheek, stood up, patted his hand and said. "Then we need to spend more time together!"

Jack looked into her eyes, smiled and quickly glanced away, stating, "Yes we must, sweety!" That was that. Jane knew beyond a shadow of doubt, Jack Prinston was no longer hers.

*

Our ace investigative reporter made her way to the "Dark Roast" coffee shop. As she drove through the noisy avenues of D.C. she reminisced about other clandestine meetings like the one she was going to. She recalled other reporters in her field and what they had to go through to get the "story." These thoughts caused her to focus on what may be ahead, just in case this thing was for real. The streets, crowded as they were, seemed to be void of life, as the thoughts of secrecy took over her reality and composed a temporary story of intrigue.

She parked her car just across the street from the coffee shop and waited. It was 3:30 PM and she would watch and wait before immersing herself into something she might regret. Being somewhat of a gumshoe, she knew better than to rush into something that could possibly be out of sync with her modus operandi. She would approach with caution.

At precisely 4 PM she entered the coffee shop and sat in the last booth in the far corner facing the door. She punched in her order of Columbian dark with foamy cream and two heaping spoonfuls of sugar on the computer-styled pad that sat on each table in the shop. And she waited. Looking around the semi crowded shop she noticed couples, some single women and one man reading a newspaper and looking like he wasn't aware of anyone else. *Could the paper reader be the "little girl" commenter?* She waited.

After her third cup of mud, she glanced down at her wrist watch/telephone and noticed that it was 5:15 PM. Just as she was about to get up and leave, her wrist telephone rang. Knowing that only a very few people had her mobile phone number, she had no hesitation answering it. It was Poker Player.

"Hello?"

"Hey, little girl, how you doing? Miss me?"

"I told you not to call me that. Why aren't you here and, hey, how did you get this number?"

"I had no intention of showing up to meet you, and I have my means of getting any number I want. You passed my test; I just wanted to know if you were serious with me about what I will tell you about the Senator's death."

"O.K., you got my attention and I'm interested in what you have to say. Now come here and let's talk."

"No, girly, I'll never meet you, but I will give you information for which you will pay me!"

"Pay, are you crazy? I don't pay kooks! Besides, where would I get the money?"

"I know you have a budget available for these sorts of things. I know that if the information you are receiving is worth it, your superiors will fork over big bucks." Poker Player fully intended to get the biggest bucks he could from this deal. Since his surveillance money dried up from the V.P. he was in need.

"Then how do I get the information?" asked our attention-grabbed reporter.

"The waiter should be coming to your booth right now. He will give you a large envelope. Take the envelope and give the waiter a 'blue'," chuckled the wily snoop.

"Say, why do I have to give him ten bucks? You should have paid him earlier!" Susan spouted with a little bit of cream coming out her nose because of frustration. She wiped it off and gave the waiter ten dollars for the envelope. He walked away laughing after seeing the cream flow from her nose.

"O.K., I got the envelope and I gave the waiter the blue; now what?"

"Read the contents and I'll call you later! After you digest the information we can talk money. See yah later!"

Poker Player hung up and Susan, still listening, looked at the envelope and then around the coffee shop for any recognition of her caller. She paid her tab, stepped out of the shop door, glanced around without noticing anyone suspicious and drove home.

Chapter

S usan couldn't wait to get to her home after receiving the envelope from the mysterious caller. She almost swerved into a parked car while reading and driving. Reading about Hanson's midnight trips to the trash area of the Bureau of Engraving and Printing was interesting to say the least. With gates opening that shouldn't, lights going off, duffle bags and boxes of champagne, she felt that there might be a story here, but where to start?

She knew enough about the vanity level in the nation's Capital, and if you wanted to get a story on someone the best way to do it was to flatter, praise, or make him or her bigger than life to the public. The politician's ego just couldn't pass up a glittering story about themselves or someone they were associated with. Since she could get into the White House press operations through her bureau chief, she knew where to start. A nice story about the late Senator Hanson could get people to open up and share about a lifetime of service to our nation. She called Lester Phillips, the White House Press Secretary.

"White House Press Office, may I help you?"

"Yes, this is Susan Collins; may I speak to Lester Phillips, please?"

"Does Mr. Phillips know you are calling?"

"No, ma'am, but he knows me."

"What should I tell him is the nature of the call?"

"I am a staff reporter with the Washington Herald, and we will be doing a story on the life and service of the late Senator Hanson. Mr. Phillips knew Senator Hanson and I'm sure would like to give us some insight to his life." Susan was rolling her eyes and puckering her lips with an "I can't believe myself" smile.

"Oh yes, I think Mr. Phillips would like to speak with you. Just a minute and I will see if he is free."

*

Chief of Staff Merrill sat in his office examining the latest polls of the President's "Un-Ad" campaign; they were impressive and indicated that everything was going as the chief executive desired. As the President's Chief of Staff it was his job to insure that every office was keeping the pressure on every constituent to maximize the popularity of this innovative approach to national prosperity. He would not take anything but perfection and hard work from every subordinate. He was tough, but not without mercy; demanding, but not without fairness; a workaholic, but not without taking time to play.

After reading the polls about the popularity of "Un-Ad," Mr. Merrill decided it was time for play. Everyone had worked very hard and deserved a little loosening of nerves and muscles. He walked out of his office, had the secretary summon his staff together and made an announcement. "I want everyone outside on the lawn, please!"

Obviously, everyone wondered what was going on, but had no idea what was to come. They were used to the boss pulling pranks and poking fun, but never knew when these little interruptions of the maddening schedule of Washington would come.

As each stepped out onto the lawn, they were given a baseball glove, bat, ball, or some other sports paraphernalia; it was time for fun! They knew what this meant; all work for the day was over, and you had to stop what you were doing and join in or else. The or else would mean you would be pestered to the point of absurdity by the Chief of State to the President of the United States, so you might as well enjoy.

*

As Susan was ushered into Lester Phillips' office she noticed many pictures on the wall behind his desk, including one with him and Senator Hanson shaking hands.

"Miss Collins, it is so nice to meet you. I've heard a lot about you and your skills as an investigative reporter; welcome to my turf!" Phillips was a five foot eleven inch, brown haired, slender man with a shy smile and friendly personality. He was the kind of guy you could talk to and maybe, even get to know, if you had the time.

"Thank you for seeing me. I know you are very busy, but I hope we can work together on some articles that my paper is going to run on the late Senator Robert Hanson." Susan found this lying necessary in order to get to the real truth that might come from her investigation into Hanson. However, she thought, *"If what my clandestine caller had to say is on the up and up, I will have a large article to write about the Senator anyway!"*

"What type of articles will you be writing about Senator Hanson and how can I help?"

"I know you were friends with the Senator and knew how he served the country. I just want to pick your brain and learn from your story what Mr. Hanson was like. You know, things that would help the country know a man of his caliber!"

"Well, Miss Collins, I knew him pretty well, but we weren't best friends or anything like that. We played golf and visited in each other's homes on a few occasions, but we never really got to know each other very deeply."

"I understand; I'll take anything I can get. You could even give it to me in writing if it would save you time. Maybe you could dictate some thoughts to your secretary or just put it on a CD for me. Whatever is most convenient for you, sir!"

"That's a good idea, it would give me some time to think about this and then put it on a CD for you. Would a week from now be soon enough?"

"Great, that would be great! I will come by then to pick it up. Oh, by the way, is there anyone else you could think of who would be able to contribute to the Senator's honor?" She almost laughed at saying this, as the Senator was not known for honor.

"Why, yes, the Vice President knew him, the President knew him very well, and the Chief of Staff. Of course there are many other Senators who knew him, obviously!"

Susan knew what she was about to ask would be the beginning or ending factor in her quest for answers about Hanson's death. "Could you make appointments with those people for me?" She smiled and looked like it was no big deal to get an appointment with the President and Vice President.

"Well, Miss Collins, they are busy people, but I think they both would like to say something nice about the Senator. I will work on getting you in to see them. I can't promise when, but I will try to make it ASAP!"

"Thank you very much, sir. I will wait for your call and that CD!" He walked her out to the secretary's office and told his secretary to remind him to make a CD about Senator Hanson and to call the President's and Vice President's offices to see about an appointment for Miss Collins.

*

By now everyone in the office of the Chief of Staff, other than one lonely clerk manning the phones, was deep into a game of softball. Everyone was yelling and screaming or just generally letting loose of his or her pent up tension. It was cathartic for some and just plain wild for others. Nevertheless, it would do for what it was intended: to make everyone feel like they were part of a team.

Merrill's impromptu little "days of fun" were infamous ,and many secretaries, office workers and important people would show up as well. On this particular day, Nora heard of the fun and came by. It was obvious from the clothes she was wearing that she was ready for play as well.

"Well, here is the 'First Lady," announced Merrill as he walked in her direction and offered her his hand. She responded by giving him hers and bowed toward the other players with a short dip at the waist and a gentle wave with her other hand. She knew the rules of these impromptu games and was ready to get involved right away.

"Is it my turn to bat?" questioned the welcomed newcomer.

"Yes!", screamed some far away voice in the outfield. "Take the heavy one and hit it outa-here!"

Nora stepped up to home base, raised the heavy bat, feet spread wide, arms raised high and chin stuck out like she meant business. "O.K. pitcher, give me your best!"

Merrill stood behind her as the umpire as well as being as close to her as possible. He would be no other place if he had the choice on any given day. He still loved her and would do anything to get her back from Jack. Although he maintained the proper decorum at all times around Nora, everyone knew he had a thing for her.

"O.K. lady, here comes my best shot." At that, the pitcher, a young, strong energetic intern threw the softball with all his might

Swoosh went the ball, across the base but a little too far to the inside and dangerously close to the First Lady's head. She jerked back, lost her balance and let loose of the bat. As she tried to keep her footing, she bumped into Merrill and they both started to lose control. He grabbed her by the waist and held tight as they went spinning around trying to maintain an upright stance, all the while her screaming, him puffing and the crowd laughing. It was a sight to behold! When they finally caught their balance, Nora was in his arms and he was looking into her eyes. No doubt there was still a connection between them, other than his arms and her grasping hands.

After they had finally maintained their composer she struck out at bat and went to the bench to wait for the next inning. When the inning ended, Richard met her at the bench, took a drink of water, and sat down beside her. She looked at him, smiled, and softly blurted out, "Richard, I am not happy with Jack. I miss you!" and then walked out onto the field to take her place. Richard sat stunned, not quite believing what he had just heard, even though it kissed his imagination and confirmed his wildest dreams.

*

Two days later Susan was informed that she had appointments with the President and Vice President on two consecutive days for twenty minutes each. She was elated but nervous, knowing that her appointments were gotten under less then truthful circumstances. She did not lose any sleep over the situation, however, as she had her appointments.

It was Monday morning and her appointment with President Prinston was for 10 AM. She was on time and waiting for the secretary to usher her into the President's office when she noticed a young man just hanging around the outer office. He looked familiar to her, but she couldn't place his face. "Nice looking," she thought. "I wonder who he is?"

"The President will see you now, Ms. Collins! Ms. Collins, the President will see you!" came the voice in her ear but out-there someplace in her mind. She was daydreaming about the cute guy she was looking at and forgot where she was. "What?" was all she said as she sleepily looked up at Jane Dean, who by now was wondering what type of kook was asking to see the President.

"Oh, I'm sorry, I must have been daydreaming!" "Please, lead the way!" She followed Jane, all the while scolding herself for her immature mind tripping over a cute young man.

"Ms. Collins, sir!"

"Come in Ms. Collins, have a seat. Would you like something to drink?" President Prinston warmly welcomed Susan.

"No thank you, Mr. President, I'm fine. Thank you very much for seeing me." Susan sat and gazed into the eyes of the one President who impressed her more than any other. In her mind he was a man of his word. He told the country what was needed and did whatever it took to deliver on his bravado. She liked a guy like that!

"Well, Ms. Collins, I guess you want to talk about Senator Hanson?"

"Yes, sir, I do! My paper will be running some articles on him in the future and we believe your input is vital. You were friends with him and seem to know a lot about him. Am I correct on that?"

"Why, yes, we were friends. He helped with my campaigns and did much to spread the word about my platform of beliefs and desires to see the country prosper. He stuck with me when many others saw me as having no chance of winning in the early days of my political career. Yes, he was a good man and a close friend!"

"Mr. President, did he have any enemies?" Susan was not known for beating around the bush and fired away with a question that would catch anyone off guard, if there were something to hide.

"Well, Ms. Collins, every politician has enemies, you know that! But, if you mean an enemy, like the hateful type, I don't think so. Why do you ask that?"

"Well, Mr. President, the accident that took his life, seemed to be, well, kind of weird!"

"We had the FBI investigate the circumstances of the accident and found it to be an accidental homicide. It seems that the tanker was stolen hours before and was in the wrong place at the right time...I mean wrong time! Sorry!"

"Yes sir, I heard all about the report of his death. I just wanted to know if he had any enemies that would do something like that?"

"I don't think he had those types of enemies, Ms. Collins. He was a good man, loyal, friendly and a hard working servant of this country." President Prinston was visibly disturbed by Susan's questions, but maintained his composure. "Is there anything else you need from me, Ms. Collins?"

"I guess that would about do it sir. If there is anything else you would like to have in the articles, you could send them to my newspaper. Thank you very much for your time, sir!" Although she knew that the interview was over, she had this feeling in her 'knower' that there would be more forthcoming about Senator Hanson from the President. She was right.

Departing the Oval Office, Susan noticed the cute guy who had captivated her earlier embarrassed thoughts. He was still there and she just had to meet him. With her usual frontal assault approach, she made straight for him.

Nathan by now had noticed Susan and fell under the same mind tripping sedative that Susan had had. He was not in the habit of gawking at girls, but this one was worth looking at. She was a petite, midnight-haired, slender woman with bright blue eyes that seemed to twinkle as she looked at you. At least that's what Nathan saw. He was captivated by her smile and straightforward approach to him. He was not intimidated by her and would soon find his mind scrambled by her every movement. To say that he was hooked would be the understatement of the century.

"Hi, I'm Susan Collins! You look familiar, and like I should know you, but I just can't place your face. Do I know you?"

"Hi, me Nathan!" was all Nathan could say, like some Neanderthal who had been caught in the headlights of a wooly Mammoth dump truck.

90

On hearing this, Susan's eyes widened as she stuck out her hand and said, "Hi me Jane!" all the while giggling and then poked Nathan in the ribs.

Nathan looked surprised and then started to laugh along with Susan. It was like they knew each other, from just one stupid verbal mistake.

"Sorry, I mean, my name is Nathan Prinston!" Nathan finally corrected himself and stuck out his hand to shake Susan's.

"I deserved that! Sorry!"

"Hey, don't apologize! That was fun!" Susan responded with a large smile and a let's continue look.

"I should have recognized you Nathan. I'm sorry!"

"That's OK. I've always tried to stay out of the public's eye and let my dad do his thing! Could I buy you lunch, dinner or anything?" Nathan said as he touched her arm and guided her out of the office area and toward the hall.

"Why, yes, I am very thirsty and a bit hungry. Where to?"

"I know this little café on fifth and thirteenth, 'The Dark Roast' coffee shop that is perfect for lunch." Nathan knew that they would not be alone, as the Secret Service agents would be tagging along. "But we'll have a bit of company with us. You know, the Secret Service guys! Do you mind?" Nathan pleaded with a please don't mind look.

"No, I don't mind. They won't sit at our table will they?"

"No, they'll be discreet, or else!" At that, they were off to start a relationship that would change lives, test allegiances and cement a bond that would forge new paths in many endeavors.

While Nathan was being ushered into new adventures and meeting people who would cast the dye for his future, his sister was being shackled by darkness that would manipulate her every thought.

Rebecca could be seen walking around the White House looking like she was trying to find something she had lost. Her eyes were glassy and her hair unkempt. She would walk up to secret agents, secretaries, or any other staff member and blurt out some off the wall remark or crazy verbiage that didn't make sense.

On many occasions, although not looking for Wannetta Morales, the maid, Rebecca would run into her. If she couldn't avoid contact, she would scream, raise her arms in a defensive manner and puke out some unintelligent words. It seemed she was afraid of Wannetta, even though Wannetta was smaller than Rebecca and was soft spoken.

Wannetta knew what the problem was. It was a demon that possessed Rebecca and hated everything about what Wannetta stood for and believed. The demon knew that his time was short and did everything possible to keep from being exposed through Wannetta's intervention.

On one of her encounters with Rebecca she had enough of the demon's attacks and accusations. Although she was nervous and not quite sure what to do, she approached Rebecca and was ready to encounter this nemesis from hell. As usual the demon, because it felt trapped, mouthed an obscene word through Rebecca. This time Wannetta, who had been prayed up, stood her ground, recalled scripture that spoke of her authority as a believer against demons, pointed her finger at Rebecca and stated, "You foul spirit of death and discord, I demand that you shut up and be quiet, in Jesus' name!" Rebecca froze in her tracks, became stone-faced, without blinking her eyes and let Wannetta pass. Wannetta, shaken, but serene, walked past the poor possessed girl and went about her business. She didn't realize she had the God-given power to cast the demandable spirit out of Rebecca. It was enough for her that the demon would not speak to her like that again.

After Wannetta left the room, Rebecca came to her senses, if that were possible, looked like she didn't know any of what had just happened, tottered down the hall, mumbling strange words and gesturing like she was talking to someone. If it weren't so sad, it would almost be comical watching poor Rebecca act like one of the Three Stooges scampering away from an encounter with madness.

*

Nathan and Susan sat in the same booth that she had when she got the information about Senator Hanson. She toyed with the idea of sharing with Nathan the information, but decided against it, just in case there was anything to it or in the event his dad knew about, she would wait.

"I hope this booth is fine with you, Susan." Nathan smilingly asked Susan.

"Why, yes, I like this booth," Susan replied with an inward smile and touch of mystery. "I've been here before. I like this place."

"Great!" is all Nathan said as he nervously fiddled with his hands, obviously happy that he was with this pretty woman. "What is it you do again?"

"I am an investigative reporter for the Washington Herald. I also do special articles on people who make the news in the Capital, as well as just plain ole newspaper reporting. You know, anything that makes the news and those who have anything to say about anything."

"Oh, that is interesting!" Nathan replied.

"Oh, 'that's interesting' is all you're going to say? I thought we were going to get to know each other here. I hope our little encounter back at the White House wasn't a mistake?" was Susan's comeback to Nathan's nervous reply.

"I'm sorry, I know I sound like a dope, but I, but I, well I mean, you make me nervous!" Nathan confessed.

"I make you nervous? Why, what have I done or said that should make you nervous?"

"It isn't anything you have said or done. It's just that... Well, you're very pretty! There, I said it!

Susan, who was now the one who couldn't put two intelligent words together said, "Oh, ah, I mean, well thank you!"

"You're welcome, Miss Collins!"

"Oh, please don't call me Miss Collins. Please call me Susan." And at that she reached across the table and caressed his hands.

Nathan gently squeezed her hands, smiled and said, "I think we just broke the ice."

"Yes, I think we have. I like your smile, Nathan."

"I like yours too."

From that moment on, Susan and Nathan began to see each other. As a new Christian, Nathan was cautious with his heart and decided to seek advice from his confidant Albert Frank in these matters.

*

The next day Nathan found Albert in the boiler room and shared with him about the heavenly meeting with Susan.

"Brother, you should see this woman. She is beautiful! She has the greatest smile! She is smart, inquisitive, and knows a lot about a lot of things."

If was obvious to Albert that Nathan had fallen for Susan and needed a guiding hand of spiritual reality, but before he could interject caution and truth Nathan spoke up again.

"Albert, I really like Susan, but I don't think she is a Christian, and I don't want to do anything that would lead me astray. Would you give me some advice in these matters, please?"

It was amazing to Albert the spiritual insight this young man had. He wished that many of his other associates had as much. He knew, however, that he had to be wise and led by the Holy Spirit to help Nathan. He said, "Yes, Nathan, I will give you some advice. If Susan is not born again, then you must not become too serious with her. You must guard your heart against becoming yoked with her, and until she turns to the Lord you must just be friends. Do you understand this?"

Nathan had the look of understanding, but you read between the lines that said, "I wish there was another way," when he replied "Yes, I know!"

"Nathan, trust God to bring about the proper relationship here. Don't get ahead of God. Rest in His timing and you will be rewarded. Let's pray!"

As they prayed, Nathan reached over and grabbed Albert's hand. When Albert finished praying, Nathan prayed, "God, I trust you in this matter. I pray for Susan, oh God. I ask that you save her and reach her heart for your glory. I ask that you help me not to fall for Susan if she is not to be in my life. I ask that you help me guard my heart, my flesh, and my emotions. You are my life and more important than anything else in life, and I don't want anything to ruin my walk with you. In Jesus name, Amen!"

Albert thought, "Here this young man comes to me for advice, but he has enough wisdom for the both of us and then some. I could learn from him!" He said, "Nathan, you are a fine young man. God has great things in store for you! I am sure glad I know you!"

*

That same day Susan had her appointment with the Vice President about his knowledge of Senator Hanson.

"Thank you for seeing me, Mr. Vice President. I'll be as brief as possible, as I know you are a busy man!"

"Well, Ms. Collins, I always have time for the press. It has been my policy to keep the press

96

informed and an open line to the public. After all, it is for the people I work!" Vice President Lambkin was sincere in these remarks, as he really thought this way.

"Sir, as you probably know, my paper will be running some articles on the life and national service of Senator Hanson. After all, he served our country for many years!"

"Yes, Ms. Collins, he was a great man. He saw to it that his constituents were served, but without sacrificing the nation's overall good." The V. P. believed these things, because they were correct. What he wasn't telling her was his secret about the investigation he had conducted on the Senator.

Susan asked the usual questions regarding how the Vice President knew Hanson and so on. You, know, the usual build up the dead guy stuff! Then she got to the main questions about his death. "Sir, do you know of any enemies the Senator had? You, know, his death was rather weird! It was almost like someone was out to get him. It was a strange thing, that gas tanker being out there on that road at that time of night. Wasn't it?" She leaned forward as she asked the "Wasn't it?" question. She didn't suspect the V. P. of any wrongdoing, but she felt this urge to press in.

Lambkin's face flushed and turned red as he replied. "Well, yes, it was rather weird, as you say. But, I think everything was investigated and there was no wrong-doing found."

"Yes, sir, I know that, but it sure was amazing how that tanker was out there. After all, gas isn't used much anymore and it sure isn't worth much, or at least it isn't used to the extent that anyone would want to steal a tanker full. I just wonder why someone would be out on that road with a tanker full of gas?" Susan was probing for some kind of a reaction, but she wasn't sure what.

"I have to admit, Ms. Collins, I agree with you about all of that. However, there wasn't any foul play found." The V. P. replied with a calmer demeanor that softened his face. He wanted to share with her his suspicions about the President and his associations with Hanson, but he just couldn't. That's all they were, suspicions without proof.

Chapter

≈10≈

"Would you like another cool drink sir?" The slender, soft spoken beach waiter asked Greely, who by now was enjoying himself, feeling somewhat safe from dangers in D.C. The breeze, sun, and ocean fragrance had a way of quieting fears and stabilizing anyone who had a past they wanted to forget. Greely could not see the waiter as he stood between him and the blaring sun.

"No thanks; I have had enough for today!"

"Would you like to order from the restaurant, sir?'

"Yes, I would like a club sandwich with very little mayo, please."

As the waiter departed, Greely noticed two seedy looking characters about twenty-five yards down the beach sitting on lawn chairs. They were not dressed for the beach and seemed to find him most interesting.

Every now and then they would turn to look at him and then speak to each other. It made Greely uneasy, but he did not find their curiosity too extreme. He was in the French Rivera, and there were always strange Frogs around. He ate his club sandwich and departed for his room.

*

Albert was working down in the basement of the White House in the same area that he was first brought to on the evening of the China Room water incident. He was back in the corner adjusting an old doorframe when he heard voices close by. It seemed to be coming right behind his head and through the wall. Although he had been in this area many times, he didn't think there was another room on the other side of that wall. He slowly made his way around the corner and followed it until the wall ended. He could still hear the voices but could not see a soul. He put his ear to the wall and listened, making out the President's voice. Keeping his ear close and touching the wall he walked along its distance until the voices became clearer. Yes, it was the President and some other voice he did not recognize. As he continued to listen, all the while touching the wall, he noticed a beam of light piercing through a crack and attacking the adjacent wall. He took the liberty of peeping into the crack and saw the President. As he did, he saw the President give a man, out of sight, what looked like a large stack of money. He couldn't be sure, but the money looked like it was a bunch of one hundred dollar bills. The yellow color was a dead giveaway.

Albert felt guilty listening in on the President of the United States, but it seemed so odd where the conversation was taking place. He listened further.

"Are you sure you know that it is him?"

"Yes sir, it's him! My man down there is sharp and doesn't make mistakes."

"Well, then, get it done!" At that moment one of the furnaces close to the wall started up and Albert could not hear the rest of what was being said.

If Albert could have heard the rest of the conversation he would have heard, "Have them make it look like a small time robbery!"

"Yes sir! It will be done as soon as possible!"

"Listen, I want it done sooner than that, I want all these loose ends taken care of fast! I can't afford someone spilling their guts by accident because of too much rum!" The President was right in the man's face and standing toe to toe.

Albert could not see the man's face but could only make out his form. He felt uneasy but figured that it was none of his business. He couldn't shake off an inner turmoil of darkness being planned by the President. He prayed silently and went about his business.

*

The night air was electric with excitement; it was holiday time and every street was filled with French vacationers enjoying the summer festivals. Greely was in the mood for fun and made his way down the stairs and out of his hotel. People were pressing all around laughing, singing, and watching the costumed party makers. It was thrilling for Greely as he had no fears, was now very rich, and felt out of sight and mind of anyone who knew what he knew.

Greely seemed to be the only one without a costume; even children were dressed up in colorful masks and the like. Just as he turned the corner, a large man dressed in a pirate's outfit knocked him off his feet. Greely went down with a thud, hitting the curb and scraping his hands on the pavement.

"Hey, man, watch out. You could really hurt someone!"

"Oh, I'm sorry, let me help you up!" was the pirate's reply as he reached down for Greely's arm. As he did, Greely noticed a thirty-eight special sticking out of the corner of his pocket.

"Hey, man, get away from me!" is all Greely could say as he quickly stood up and started to walk away. The pirate slowly walked in Greely's direction, all the while supposedly trying to calm him down. Greely, by now, was afraid and would have none of the pirate's sympathy. He began to walk faster.

"Hey, come back, let's talk about it!"

"Leave me alone!"

"Come on, friend, I'm sorry, I didn't mean nothing!"

Greely by now was trotting and so was the pirate, up one street and down another. No matter where Greely went the pirate was there. He was like a dark mass of unknown hate that had the speed of a leopard and the mind of a compass pointing north no matter what, and Greely was north.

Just as Greely got around the last corner and into the street that led to his hotel, he noticed the pirate ahead of him. *"How could this be?"* He thought, as the pirate was behind him. The hateful adversary may have been fast, but he wasn't that fast. As Greely stood there looking up ahead at the pirate he heard steps behind him. Turning, he saw the pirate again! Mind screaming, fear taking over and his feet incapable of moving made Greely a whimpering pup. As he turned around to try to run again he noticed that there were two pirates. Identical twins of bearded trouble! They grabbed him and took him to his room, all the while telling people who noticed, that he was a friend that had had too much to drink.

The next morning he was found with a thirty-eight special bullet hole in his head and lying on top of Greely was the body of a man dressed in a pirate's costume. He had been shot in the back. Although the murderer or murderers were never found, it looked like a robbery because both men's wallets were missing and any valuables they both had on them.

---
*

Others met the same fate as Greely and the pirate. In the small town of Reidsville, Georgia, a man was found with a bullet hole in his head, also. It seemed that a Mr. James Cobb, who had not too long ago retired from The Bureau of Printing and Engraving, was found dead, lying on a bank of the Ohoopee River. According to the Sheriff's Office, the murder of Mr. Cobb looked like a robbery. No suspects were named and the investigation was at a stand still!

---
*

Months Pass

————————— * —————————

Susan wrote the newspaper article about Senator Hanson with the usual flattery, but not much about the way he died. She just mentioned the tragic way he died, the rather odd gas tanker being on the road, but could not go into any detail about the information she had received from Poker Player.

Poker Player did call again, only to inquire about what her investigation had uncovered, but nothing else. Susan figured that his information was at an end and agreed to give him the $2,000.00 that her superiors had authorized. She asked him to contact her every now and then, just in case he might come up with something else.

————————— * —————————

By now Susan and Nathan were seeing each other on a regular basis and their lives were becoming intertwined. He could only think of her, and she found it very difficult concentrating on work. He was maintaining a 3.5 average at college and was soon to graduate with a degree in Social Development. She was considered the top Reporter at her newspaper and earned top pay. Her life was good but had an inner sense of darkness that she could not shake. She knew why the inner turmoil was there. Ever since she had been seeing Nathan and listening to his talk of God and eternity there was this need within her for an inward change. The change and confrontation of things that really matter came to a head one evening with Nathan.

Nathan had been praying about "closing the deal," as he called it, with Susan. "Closing the deal" would be a focused conversation with Susan about her eternal life and where she stood with Christ. She always listened to him with rapt attention and many times commented in the positive. He felt that she was ready for the direct approach and believed that God had set the stage for this hour.

Nathan asked Susan to come to the White House, as he wanted her to see something. When she arrived, they went up to the Presidential residence so that Nathan could introduce her to his parents. By now, Susan had met the President many times, but as yet had not met Nathan's mother or sister. She was nervous, but looked cool and calm, and was keenly aware of her surroundings.

"Dad and Mom, I would like you to meet Susan Collins," Nathan formally said as he introduced Susan.

"Yes, I have met Miss Collins before. That was a very nice article on Senator Hanson you wrote, Susan!"

"Thank you, sir! It is very nice seeing you again, Mr. President." She moved closer to Jack and Nora.

"It is so very nice meeting you, Susan. Nathan has mentioned you so often. I feel like I know you already," Nora said as she met Susan and put her arm around the young women.

"Susan, this is Rebecca, my sister."

"Hi, Rebecca, I have heard much about you from your brother. He thinks the world of you!" Susan was telling the truth, as Nathan had mentioned Rebecca many times to her. He loved his sister and knew that she was under direct influence of demons. Although he didn't tell Susan about the demons, he did tell her of her emotional problems and dark encounters that he knew of.

Rebecca look surprised and relieved, as she surmised that her whole family thought she was crazy. She turned, looked at Nathan and saw something she never saw before, love. It was a rare moment for her, as the demons did not respond in the presence of Nathan. They knew his relationship with Christ and his potential as a believer. It was in their best interest not to show up at this moment with a child of God who knew scripture.

"Well, we are going to spend some time together. I'm going to show Susan around the White House and just hang out." Nathan said as he directed Susan out of the living room and towards his room.

"Nice meeting y'all!" is all Susan could say as she was directed out of the room.

Jack, Nora, and Rebecca just laughed as Nathan maneuvered Susan away.

"Nathan, that was not nice. You didn't give them time to talk to me."

"Yes, yes, I know, I want you to see something great!" At that, he directed Susan through his room and over to the window.

"Look at that sight!" Nathan acting like a tour guide grabbed the curtain and threw it back. With one swift move of the curtain the lights of Washington, D.C., the monuments, the trees, and the grandeur of it all flooded the room.

"Oh, it's beautiful!" Susan exclaimed as she leaned closer to the window and gazed in awe. "I have seen this city from many vantage points throughout my years here, but never from this site, from this perspective, and with someone like you!" She turned to Nathan and gave him a kiss on the cheek.

"Hey, that was nice. Now come with me, I want to show you something else!" Nathan said, as he put his hand to the spot where Susan had kissed it and smiled.

Nathan led Susan down and out of the residence, into every room in the White House and explained every facet of the grand building. Its history, drama, and importance to the free world were commented on as he gave her his own tour and insight.

"Now, I want to take you someplace special!" With a twinkle in his eyes and gentle holding of her hand, Nathan guided her down some stairs into the basement.

They entered what looked like a storage room with many shelves containing boxes and other items that didn't look like they were used much. Nathan walked over to one set of shelves in the corner of the room, picked up the bottom shelf, and gave a tug. The shelf moved up, and the whole set of shelves moved toward Nathan and then to the left, revealing a room behind them.

"I found this room one day when I was snooping around," Nathan said with a smile and come here gesture.

They both entered the room and Nathan pulled the shelves closed behind them. Susan objected, but Nathan reassured her that it was O.K.

"I come here quite often just to think. It is like my own little hiding place," Nathan said as he took Susan's hand and motioned to her to sit next to him on a couch that had been there for years.

The room had a small 40-watt light bulb hanging in the center but nothing else other than the couch. There were a few cracks in the wall and one through which you could see a sliver of light coming through from the other side. Susan got up and peeked through the crack. She saw what looked like a small repair room. It had plumbing tools and other fix up equipment in it. She returned to her seat next to Nathan.

"This is some place you have here, Nathan I like places like this. It reminds me of my grandmother's home in Georgia. She has a place in the basement like this one. I used to go there every chance I had to be alone. I did a lot of thinking there when I was younger."

"What would you think of when you were in that room, Susan?" Nathan said with an idea in his heart where he wanted this conversation to go.

"Well, I would think of the future, dolls, boys, school, and other great important things! You know, the usual girly things!"

"What were your thoughts about the future?"

"I would wonder if I would have a future for one thing. Everyone was talking about another nuclear war with Babylon (Iraq). I was frightened!" She leaned in and grabbed Nathan's arms and put them around her.

"I was young then, and didn't give it much thought. I guess when your father is a politician you are always hearing about wars and the like. I didn't think much about anything then except school and soon being able to drive." Nathan pulled Susan closer and put his head next to hers.

"Susan, what are your thoughts about the future now? What do you think about eternity?" He felt so calm, and under the leading of the Holy Spirit that he got right to the reason for bringing Susan to his secret place.

"Well, since I have been seeing you I have thought a lot about it. You seem to touch my very core when you talk about God, peace, love and surrender to His ways. It is like you know him personally and very intimately. It is so wonderful!" She pushed in closer so she could feel Nathan's chest and heart.

"What do you think you need to do about those feelings and thoughts? It is not me touching your very core, it is God. He is speaking to you through me. He loves you and wants you to know Him. Your life has been directed to this very moment so that you could give Him supremacy over it. He wants you to trust Him for your future, live for Him every hour, and share with Him all that you are. Can you do that, Susan?"

"I think I can, I want too, I need to, I…" And with that she began to cry, turning to Nathan for support. He in turn held her at arms length. He didn't want just human emotions to dictate this special time. It was all too easy in these types of moments to let emotions take over and the spirit to be lost. Nathan wanted nothing but spiritual truth, the presence of God, and the leading of the Holy Spirit in this circumstance. Susan would have to come to Jesus from her heart, not her head. She must see her total need for Christ and her undeserving human nature that lives for sin.

"Susan, Jesus paid the price for your sins and wrong lifestyle. He wants you to understand your lost position without Him and what He did on the cross for you. Do you understand this?" Nathan was nervous as he spoke so forcefully to the one person in his life that meant the most.

"Yes, I think I do! But, Nathan, I am not the person you think I am. I have sinned, I have had bad thoughts, done wrong things, went to the wrong places, I, I..." She lowered her head and sobbed. Nathan pulled her closer, but not too close, he wanted this to be a moment of understanding and nothing else.

She continued.

"Oh I need Jesus, Nathan! I need Jesus!" She had seen her need and realized the remedy.

"Well then, Susan, Jesus is ready to receive you unto Himself. It is a matter of your will, your surrender, and your obedience to God's will. Do you understand that?" Nathan asked as he lifted her chin in order for her to see his face and eyes.

"Tell Him what is in your heart right now!"

Susan pulled away from Nathan, stood to her feet as if to leave, but then got down on her knees to pray. She sank down, sat on her heels and cried out to God. Time flew by in that dimly lit room as Susan poured her heart and life out to God. She held nothing back. Everything and anything she could think of she repented of. Even things in her life that anyone else would have seen as minor was open before God and her Savior. She wanted no wall, vice, or darkness to stand between her and the Lord who died for her. Afterwards, it seemed like that little 40-watt bulb shown as if it were a 100-watter.

"How do you feel, honey?" Nathan said, as he caught himself using a term of endearment that he had never used before.

"I feel clean, light, and so welcomed by God! It is as if I have lost two hundred pounds of darkness!" She looked at Nathan and threw her arms around his neck. And then she said. "Nathan, I love you!"

Nathan was so surprised by her declaration that he didn't quite know what to say. He felt the same toward Susan, but didn't want this moment to be lost in the midst of everything else that had just happened.

"I love you too, Susan!" was all Nathan said, but Susan knew it was from his heart, his head, and his whole being.

They were unaware of the time as they left the "secret place," closed the hidden door, and departed the room. Going up the steps, they met Albert coming down. It was six in the morning and Albert was coming in early to fix a faulty outlet that would be needed that day in the State Dining Room.

"Hey, Albert, I have wonderful news for you. Susan has just turned to the Lord. She has come under conviction of sin and repented unto salvation. She is one of us now!" Nathan blurted out his joy and exclamation of truth not realizing that Albert and Susan had never met.

"Wonderful, wonderful, thank you, Jesus!" Albert said with genuine thankfulness, joy, and exuberance.

"Hi, I'm Albert Frank, we have never met before! Although I have heard so much about you, it is truly my pleasure meeting you!" Albert looked at Nathan and winked!

"Oh, I'm sorry! Albert, Susan, Susan, Albert, my good friend and brother in the Lord!" Nathan said with a touch of embarrassment in his voice.

"Wonderful meeting you also, Albert. I too have heard much about you. Nathan speaks of you often. I guess we are kinfolk now. You know, sister and brother in Jesus!" Susan's smile, greeting, and warmth touched Albert and he knew he had a new friend besides new spiritual kinfolk.

*

Nora found any excuse she could to visit the Chief of Staff. Most often she acted like she needed to know the President's schedule and the Chief of State was the one who would know best. She wasn't fooling anyone as his staff, her staff, and even the clean-up people knew her intentions.

"Is Mr. Merrill available to see me?" asked Nora of the Chief of Staff's secretary.

His secretary knew by now to let the President's wife in to see her boss anytime she wanted. She rang Mr. Merrill and was instructed to let Mrs. Prinston in.

As Nora entered the room, Richard met her in the center of the room and took her hand. "It is so good to see you again, Nora. I have been thinking about you so often."

"I too have been thinking a lot about you Richard. It seems like my days have no sunshine in them without a visit with you!" Nora said, taking Richard's other hand and squeezing both of them softly.

"Richard, I know I have not been very discrete with my feelings toward you. I know that others talk about us seeing each other here so often, but I just can't help myself. Jack doesn't show me any love, give me any support, or act like he even cares. It's that little tart Lora Warner; Jack sees her as much as he can. I know that they are not behaving themselves!"

"Yes, Nora, I think you're correct in your observations. Lora does spend a lot of time with Jack. I can't say anything about their behavior, however. I am loyal to Jack and wouldn't say or do anything to hurt him, but he isn't treating you fairly." Richard spoke clearly, slowly, and used his words carefully. He didn't want to run ahead in his relationship with Nora if she was not where he was in it.

"Do you think there is any chance for Jack and me to make our marriage work again, Richard?" The question took Richard by surprise! He decided to step into this troubled water with abandonment, tell Nora the truth as he saw it, and let her know how he felt!

"No, I don't, Nora! I think Jack is past the point of caring. I think you should try to find happiness elsewhere." He had not only stepped into the water, but he was up to his neck!

"I think you are right, Richard, but I am going to give it one more try. I know Jack and I have had an unwritten agreement about seeing other people in the past, but I must give our marriage one more try! I will see!" She looked at Richard, smiled, kissed his cheek and walked out.

"I am here for you if you need me, Nora!" is all Richard could say.

*

The morning was bright, warm, and breezy as Jane made her way to her office. She too had been thinking about Jack. She had been having thoughts of trying to win Jack back from Lora Warner. *"After all,"* she thought, *"before Lora came back into Jack's life I was number one!"* It didn't dawn on her that Jack had not given her a second thought after seeing Lora again.

Jane made a fresh pot of Amarillo Dark Roast for Jack, ordered those special rolls he liked and insured that the page he always went to first was opened for him in the newspaper. She made sure she was wearing the bright yellow dress he had bought for her a few years ago and had just the right amount of his special perfume on. She was going to make the right impression, draw his attention to her person and body, and do the right things. Her plan was hatched and she was up to the task, to win the love of her life back. As she opened the door to the President's office she did not see him.

"Good morning Mr. President!" No answer!

"Hello!" Still no answer!

She walked over to the door leading to the small kitchenette, just outside the Oval Office. As she opened the door slowly she was hit with the scene of Jack and Lora kissing! Her mind went wild, but she held her breath, bit her tongue, and slowly closed the door and backed away. They did not see, hear, or even know anyone had seen them.

Jane went into the Ladies Room and cried quietly in a stall. Her dream was shattered, her future seemed gray, and her hate was building.

*

Nora had about the same plan in mind as Jane did. She was going to show Jack that she still cared. She knew that her work was cut out for her, but it was worth a try. After all, Jack was at one time her best friend and lover.

That evening she instructed the White House Chef to make Jack's favorite dish of prime rib, smothered in mushrooms, special garlic sauce, small potatoes, and Baked Alaska! She made sure that Rebecca would be out of the White House seeing a movie. Her attire would be everything Jack liked, would catch his attention, and draw him in. The perfume she wore cost $2,000.00 a bottle, had the aroma of heaven, and could intoxicate the senses.

It was eight o'clock when Jack came up to the residence. He was tired and hungry, but open to conversation.

"I'm home!"

"Hi, honey, I'm in the kitchen!" she called.

As he entered the room, she asked, "How'd your day go, my man?"

"Same ole, same ole, you know, just running the country!" He walked up behind Nora and patted her on the shoulder.

"Need a drink or something? The food is ready to be served at the table. I will be right there!" As Jack went to the dining room, Nora followed, bringing the salad.

They sat and began to eat. You could tell that Jack was enjoying the prime rib as he had two portions. Their small talked revolved around some politics and minor White House problems, but didn't really focus on their marriage.

Since Nora had other things in mind than small talk and politics she asked if Jack liked the dress she was wearing. His reply revealed what was in his heart.

"Yes, Lora it's very nice. I really like that yellow on you!" He didn't realize he had called Nora, Lora. But, Nora did!

"Nora, Jack, Nora! You called me Lora!" Nora's acclamation came with hurt eyes.

"I'm sorry Nora; it was an honest mistake, as I saw Lora Warner today at the office. She was there discussing that Old Growth Consortium thing!" Jack tried to look calm and collective.

"O.K. Jack, I understand!"

"Say, that sure was a great meal. You had everything I like. What's the occasion?"

"I don't know, honey, I just thought we needed to spend some time together. We haven't seen each other very much and you have been so busy!" Nora stood up, grabbed Jack's hand and directed him to the couch. As they sat down, she moved his hand up and around her neck.

Jack responded to Nora's maneuvering and obliged her desires. They stayed on the couch for about two hours, talking, drinking wine, and smooching until it was time for bed.

Nora went to the bedroom to prepare for bed and Jack went to turn off the lights in the kitchen and dining room.

"I will be with you in just a moment, honey, I need to make a call. About business, you know." Jack went to the den to use that phone.

Jack was a brave man, calling Lora from his home phone, but, when you think about it, he really didn't care.

"I know, I miss you too, you can't imagine what I just had to go through. She insisted on having a quiet evening at home, with candles, and talk on the couch. I did my best to maintain my composure, but I don't think she suspected anything!" Jack had called Lora Warner and was sharing his evening with her. He didn't realize that Nora had picked up the phone in the bedroom to listen in. She had been in the habit of doing this since Jack had been seeing Lora again. Nora's fears were confirmed, and she felt like an idiot for thinking she could win Jack back. Her hurt turned to anger and then rage as she stomped out of the bedroom and into the den.

"You are the lowest of the low, Jack. You pretended to enjoy yourself with me and then you call Lora. What a fool I have been. Don't you have honor?"

"I'm sorry, Nora, what can I say. What are you so mad about? We have had the arrangement for years! Why are you so upset now?" Jack was just living his life as he always lived it with Nora, or at least for the past nine years. He felt like their lives were separate, but with a mutual agreement to be married for the children's sake. He forgot that the children were now adults themselves.

"Well, Jack, the agreement may have been O.K. for awhile, but I thought it was about time for us to try again! Don't you want a fresh start with me?" Nora by now was in tears and looking at Jack with hope in her eyes.

"Nora, I don't want to hurt you, but no, I don't want a fresh start with you. Can't we just let things be the way they were until I leave Office? Then we can get a divorce and go our own ways?"

Nora was livid as she heard Jack's words, realized the truth, and watched his body language. She knew the reality of the situation now! She looked at Jack, raised her fist to strike at him, but then stopped and said, "Fine!" Her words said fine, but her eyes said hate, and death.

Chapter

≈11≈

It had been six months since Susan had given her life to Christ and had been living a totally different lifestyle. Her every free moment was taken up with Nathan and church. They had found a little non-denominational church, "Christian Life Fellowship Church," on the outskirts of D.C. and were very much involved with its family atmosphere.

Susan had been thinking of her grandmother's house in Georgia ever since the night in the White House when she had turned her life to Christ. She reminisced about the quiet basement room where she had spent many hours thinking about girly things: her future, dolls, boys, school, and other important matters. That room seemed to be calling her, no, pulling at her soul, to come visit. She hadn't seen her grandmother for five years and figured it would be great having her meet Nathan.

Nathan had graduated with honors by now and was taking time off to relax and enjoy his time with Susan. Although he had no job, he was living off bonds that he had cashed in. His father, although not a caring dad, had enough sense when Nathan and Rebecca were born to buy savings bonds for them. Jack had bought a $200.00 bond each month until they both reached the age of eighteen. Nathan had cashed in some of those bonds and was using them to support himself until he could find a job.

Susan had arranged for Nathan and herself to take the Maglev train from D.C. to Savannah and then rent a car from there to Reidsville, Georgia.

The Maglev train had been operating for five years and was the fastest things attached to the Earth. Its top speed was 300 mph and cruised at 250 mph. Centered and elevated in the median of Interstate 95, it was just a blur as it passed cars on the interstate. There was little noise from the Maglev other than the sound of the wind trying to get out of its way. It was a marvel of technology with its powerful electric magnets turning on and off pulling the massive metal object forward. You couldn't feel any bumps, friction, or any of the other normal train motions. As the magnets pulled the train forward, it also lifted it just a few inches above the center track. It was fast, safe, cheap, and one of the things that had come out of the Un-Ad campaign.

As they arrived in Savannah there was an air of excitement mingled with the fresh flowered mimosa that was rooted just off the platform. Its aroma greeted each passenger and seemed to whisper, "Welcome to the South!"

They collected their luggage and rented a Chevy Trailblazer with special off-road tires and extended fuel cell capacity. As they drove down Abacorn and then on out to Highway 204 toward Reidsville, they noticed the tall, overhanging trees and the wafting Spanish moss that clung to many branches. The welcoming feeling of this sight was a typical response from an unsuspecting newcomer as they drove under this canopy of glory.

Reidsville, which was seventy miles from Savannah, welcomed them with its own roofed beauty. It seemed these Live Oaks, Pecans, and other assorted trees all welcomed nature's hanging hair that clung, adorned, and completed their display of grandeur.

Reidsville was a small town with a proud history that found its memories in the Civil War, segregation, integration, and modern engineering that included all of its citizens. Its newspaper, "The Tattnall Journal," had been publishing from its inception in 1879 by the Rhoden family. The town had produced war heroes, famous sheriffs, senators, and other interesting characters that made up its own story within the grand collection that made Georgia what it was.

Taking Highway 56 out of town, Nathan and Susan passed old gas stations that had succumbed to the low prices when gasoline no longer fueled the internal combustion engine. Old homes, picturesque, dilapidated mansions, and rundown farmsteads dotted Highway 56 as they trekked their way to Susan's grandmothers.

As they turned left off the asphalt highway onto the red Georgia clay country road, Susan was obviously in a little girl mode. She had a smile from ear to ear with a glow of anticipation that radiated her remarkable beauty. It was just that beauty which attracted Nathan.

The road paralleled the Ohoopee River on the right side and farmland on the other. Cattle slowly munching grass, birds chirping, squirrels flickering here and there, and vultures flying high in the sky bombarded Susan's memory as she took in every familiar scene. It was in these settings that she played, found her knight in shining armor, and made mud pies from the red clay of youth. Her grandmother, or Mema as she was called, took time to play, educate, and mold her thinking in this hot muggy environment.

As they turned the last curve in the road leading up to the small house on the hill overlooking the river, Susan insisted on walking the rest of the way. She asked Nathan to park the Trailblazer off the road and walk with her. She wanted to enjoy the approach to the house as she had many times before. Nathan could not blame her, as the road meandered through large oak trees with the Spanish moss hanging here and there, wild flowers on each side of the road, and a hint of wisteria caressing the nostrils. It was relaxing, welcoming, and right out of someone's imagination of peace.

Nathan's mind went wild with the sight of Susan's face radiating like an angel of love. Her beauty captivated him, yes, but much more than that, he was captivated by "HER"! Her inward beauty of goodness, acceptance, and forgiveness drew him into a place of comfort and oneness with her. He knew he had to have her as his wife! Now that she was a Christian his decision was much easier. He decided to wait for the right moment, whether it was here or in the future only God knew, as he would wait on God to direct.

As they approached the house, Me-ma came running out of the front door, and with a gentle squeal from her eighty-eight year voice grabbed Susan and pulled her into her frail framed breast. There was no escaping it, Me-ma loved Susan very much, and Susan was totally captivated by her Me-ma. With tears flowing, joyful laughter, and words too happy to understand, they both collapsed on the ground. What a homecoming!

---
*

Jack Prinston sat in the Oval Office thinking about all that had transpired since he had started the Green Paper shenanigans. He had all the money he ever wanted, was President of the most powerful nation on the Earth, was messing around with beautiful women, and seemly accepted by many, but he was shallow. *"Shallow, that was it!"* he surmised as he took stock of his life.

"What's missing in my life? Why do I feel so empty? What must I do to get relief from this dry, dull, pain of heart and mind?" These thoughts came from a much forgotten recessed area of his subconscious. They were present only when he was not being bombarded by the demands of his office and most prevalent when he thought of his son. These things were odd for him since he usually never thought of his family unless they put some kind of demand on him. Other than that, they were just another means to an

end. His life was his and no one much mattered that didn't provide for his future.

Nevertheless, here he was thinking about his son. *"Let's see now, what was it that Nathan was saying when we were swimming that day months ago? Something about God, sin, peace...Yes, that was it, peace! That's what I want, peace! I need peace! I got to have peace! But, how?"*

Somewhere in the unseen areas of the highly-lighted office came a voice. It was just audible to anyone who was in the right frame of life to hear it. Only those who had given themselves over to the darker side of eternity by their lifestyle would hear the low, but muffled voice of this sinister being. Jack's lifestyle made him a prime receptor for this nemesis of light.

The eerie voice came from without, but could only be heard from within. It slowly lingered its warning and verbal direction with a touch of friendly persuasion and said, *"Don't give it much thought! You have enough to be worried with. You can't risk everything you ever worked for on these types of matters. Peace of heart and mind is what you make it! Get all you can now, for later doesn't matter! After all, Nathan is just a kid, what does he know? He is just going through a phase!"*

Just then the intercom on Jack's desk rang. It startled Jack and caused him to stop listening to the dark unseen voice. He thought he was just daydreaming, but he couldn't shake the thought that he was listening to a real person outside himself. But as he listened, he heard this other voice from within state, *"Don't let this go, come back to Nathan and his words later!"* This voice was welcoming and peaceful! With that he answered the intercom.

———————— * ————————

Picking herself up and then Me-ma, Susan was beside herself as she caressed, held hands, and then hugged the object of her affection. Nathan was amazed watching the love flow between these two different generations. He had never observed this type of affection in all of his life. His parents, grandparents, and adult friends never displayed emotion to this degree. It would just be out of place for people of their stature. Nathan, however, was cut from a different time. He was a descendant of his great, great grandfather, Abraham Prinston. Although there wasn't much information on Abraham Prinston, the one thing that was known, was that he was an itinerant preacher. It was from Abraham's prayers that Nathan had been saved! Why Jack never succumbed to the truth that had to be passed down, only God knew. Suffice it to say, Nathan was open to truth and change.

"Me-ma, I want you to meet my friend, Nathan Prinston." Susan squeezed Me-ma's hand as she took Nathan's hand and squeezed at the same time.

"I am so pleased to meet you, Nathan; Susan has bored me to tears telling me all about you over the telephone." Me-ma winked at Nathan and smiled at Susan.

"Oh, Me-ma, you are just terrible. I told you those things to help you go to sleep! You shouldn't tell

Nathan, however!" Then both Me-ma and Susan looked at Nathan and laughed.

"Well, I guess I am pleased to meet you! Ah, what should I call you? Me-ma, granny, old lady, or what?" He then looked at both of them and smiled.

"You got us there, Nathan. Please call me Rose! That's my name." With that, she reached over and hugged Nathan.

"Come in the house and let's have some iced tea!" Me-ma said as she took both Susan and Nathan by the arms and walked between them to the house.

The three of them sat on the porch of the old white house, drank iced tea, and took in the picturesque view of the Ohoopee River as it trickled its way down to the Altamaha River to the south. Nathan thought to himself in this setting, *"I hope heaven will be something like this!"*

They sat there for hours, Susan sharing the life she had had with her grandmother after her mother had died giving her birth and her father had left for another life. He couldn't handle taking care of Susan after his wife died and just left the task up to his mother. Darrell Collins wasn't much of a homebody and emotionally couldn't handle the thought of raising a child on his own. So, Rose Collins was given the charge of Susan, which she welcomed and never regretted.

Rose's husband, Taylor, died of cancer soon after Susan came to live with them. Susan helped take up the vacant spot in Rose's heart and eased the pain of loneliness. It was difficult, but worth the many years she had with Susan. When Susan left for D.C. and college it was tough on Rose, but a decision she knew was right.

Nathan and Susan spent three days at Me-ma's house. They took in the sights of Reidsville, went swimming in the Ohoopee, and took many walks down secret paths that Susan had known. The days were warm with blue skies, powdery white clouds that softly floated by, and setting sunlight that enhanced their love.

Nathan had come to the point that he knew that he wanted Susan as his wife. Every night while he lie in bed, in the room next to Susan's, with their headboards separated by three and one half inches of drywall, insulation and paint, he would daydream of his life with her. It was agonizing knowing she was so close, but yet so far from him. He didn't want this separation any more; she had to be his wife.

Each night he prayed for God's timing for his marriage to Susan. He didn't want to rush things, but also reminded God that he was only human! On the last night, he prayed again and got an answer. It came in the form of scripture and God spoke clearly and precisely through His word. It stated, *"Who can find a virtuous woman? for her price is far above rubies. The heart of her husband doth safely trust in her, so that he shall have no need of spoil. She will do him good and not evil all the days of her life."* Then in his soul he heard *"You have found your wife!"*

He lay in bed with tears running down his face with joy and thankfulness. The moon was full and the light of its brilliance flooded his room like a confirmation of the words he had just heard. He knew where those verses were found in scripture and jumped up and got his Bible. Flipping through the Old Testament with the lights off was easy, as moonlight made every word stand out like a beacon for a searching soul. Yes, there they were in Proverbs thirty-one, verses ten through twelve. *"A virtuous woman! Yes, that's it, she is a virtuous woman! Since Susan has come to Jesus, she has been a virtuous woman. I trust her and I love her. She is the woman for me!"* With that he drifted off to sleep with the plan of asking her to marry him in the morning.

Me-ma, stuck her head into Susan's room and quietly called, "Susan, it's time for breakfast!"

Susan rolled over, smiled, raised her arms above her head and stated, "Yes, it's morning, it's breakfast, and another wonderful, new beginning and faith adventure!"

"Well, aren't we the bubbly person today! You must have had a wonderful rest." Me-ma replied as she closed the door and started for Nathan's room.

She didn't make more than three steps before Nathan's door opened and out came the bright eyed, dressed, ready for anything young man. "Good morning, Rose! How are you today?" He grabbed her and gave her a peck on the cheek and a pat on her shoulder.

"My, my, my, my, my that full moon must have done something special last night on those two!" was all Rose could say.

---------- * ----------

The Franks and Moraleses had become close friends over the many months that Albert had been working at the White House. They spent time together on cookouts, came to attend the same church, and gathered together for prayer weekly.

On this particular evening as they gathered for their weekly prayer meeting, Albert asked for a special prayer for Nathan and Susan. They all knew that Nathan and Susan had gone away together to visit her grandmother, but Albert felt that something was about to happen that was very important. He didn't have a thought about their marriage, only that something important was up. He asked the group to pray for the couple.

Each person in the prayer group took their turn lifting up Nathan and Susan and what might be happening in their lives. Only toward the end of the prayer session was prayer worded about marriage. It came from a very unpresuming person, little Virginia Morales. This eight-year-old soft-spoken and quiet child slowly cleared her throat and began, "Dear God, I ask you to help Nathan and Susan serve you as you lead them. Keep them safe and from any hurt! Amen!" But just before the group ended, Virginia blurted out, "Oh, by the way God, help Nathan ask Susan to marry him! Amen, again!" That was that, a prayer for marriage. Everyone in the room just sat there, silent and with a shy smile on their faces.

------------ * ------------

After breakfast, Susan asked Nathan to go for a walk with her to a special place. Growing up, Susan had made many special places in the surrounding

129

indents along the river, but there was one she held extra special.

As they walked along the path which led south along the river they held each other's hand and spoke of the beauty of Me-ma's world.

"There was no doubt about it; this would be a wonderful place to raise children!" Nathan mentioned as they slowly made their way to Susan's special place.

"So, you like children?" Susan replied.

"Yes, I think kids would be wonderful. I'm kind of a kid myself at heart you know. Having a playmate would be great!"

"Oh, Nathan, get serious!"

"I am serious, I would love children!"

Just then Susan yanked Nathan's hand as she started to run off the path and into a densely-packed stand of trees, weeds, and brush.

"Come, Nathan, look!" Susan exclaimed with delight as they broke through the wall of nature and entered into what looked like a room of color.

The special place was a cleared out patch of grass, in the center of trees, with little room between each. Beyond the trees and between every possible place of escape were weeds, brush, flowers, and other plantings of nature that was put there by someone. That someone had to be Susan when she was young. Sure the place needed some clearing, but for the most part it was a sanctuary of peace. Wild flowers grew everywhere and just off in the east corner sat a bench with arm rests.

"Wow!" was all Nathan could say.

"Do you like it, Nathan?"

"Do I like it? It is great! This is wonderful, this is perfect, and this is the place!" With that, he took Susan by the arm, led her to the bench, sat her down, and got down on one knee!

"Susan, I love this place! It speaks of you! It reflects your beauty, both outwardly and inwardly! It draws me in and calls me to rest! It welcomes my presence and accepts my person! It speaks of love!" Susan looked at Nathan with a little bit of wonderment, much love, and some surprise!

Nathan continued. "Sweetheart, I know that we have not known each other for a great amount of time. But I believe I know you enough! I have prayed, sought God, and believe I have heard from Him!"

Susan put her right hand up to Nathan's mouth with a gentle caress and a "be still" with her other left index finger over her own lips and said, "Yes, Nathan, I will marry you!"

Nathan couldn't contain himself and threw his arms around Susan and kissed her with a passion that came from his very center.

"But how did you know that is what I was going to ask you?" Nathan mouthed, but with very little sound coming forth.

"Well, sweetheart, I too have been praying about our future. Last night in my room, with the brilliance of the moonlight coming into it, I prayed and asked God to speak to me about marriage. He spoke through his word and told me, *'For this reason a man will leave his father and mother and be united to his wife, and the two will become one flesh. However, each one of you also must love his wife as he loves himself, and the wife must respect her husband.'* I believe we were meant to be together!"

"Me too! Last night God told me, through His word, that we were to be married. In Proverbs thirty one, verses ten through twelve, He told me that I had found my wife!" They looked at each other, tears running down their faces and wetting the arm of the bench. The outdoor setting for this once in a lifetime event could not have been better. The birds were chirping, the flowers giving off their aroma, and the light from the morning sun was spotlighting special flowers as it impacted "their special place"!

It must have been close to noon when they decided to return to Me-ma's house. Running along the path leading back to the house was an exercise in stamina, as ever so often they would stop, kiss, hug and laugh. This went on until they reached the house, swung open the door, and burst into the kitchen. They found Me-ma returning from the lunch table after setting the places for one of her home cooked meals.

"I was just fixin to call you two for lunch. I have made fried chicken, black-eyed peas, rice, gravy, and cornbread, my special last day meal for you two. I hope you are hungry!" She said with a granny smile and look of welcome.

"Me-ma, we are hungry, but first we have something to tell you!" Susan blurted out with a grin and gentle nudging on her grandmother's arm as she guided her to sit down.

Me-ma accepted the chair all the while smiling and enjoying the joy and happiness on Susan and Nathan's faces. She may have been eighty, but she wasn't ignorant to moments like this and the atmosphere it created around two people who have made "decisions."

"Me-ma, Nathan has asked me to marry him, and I have accepted!" Susan beamed as she shared her joy with the only person on earth who should know these things before anyone else!

Me-ma threw her hands up to her mouth, looked at Susan, then to Nathan and then back to Susan. Her face said everything that was in her heart, but managed to whisper out, "Oh, Susan, I am so happy for you both! This is right! I have been praying for God's guidance for you two!"

Me-ma pulled Susan to her breast and gave her a motherly hug that gave its own approval. She then reached out to Nathan and did the same thing.

Nathan felt the warmth of Rose's love and the acceptance of her countenance. However, he realized that since Susan's father was nowhere to be found, he should at least ask Me-ma for Susan's hand in marriage. He knew it was after the fact, but nevertheless, it should be done.

"Rose, I know that this is a little late, but since Susan's father isn't here, I need to ask you for Susan's hand in marriage. I love her with my whole heart. I will take care of her and treat her with the utmost respect and honor." He looked longingly into Rose's face waiting for approval.

"Oh, Nathan, I can't imagine Susan having a better husband than you. Yes, a thousand times over!" was all Rose could say as she wiped away tears from her eyes!

"My, my, my, my, my, my, my, there I go letting loose of happy juice for all to see!" Rose exclaimed as the three of them cried for joy.

Susan could hardly contain herself after hearing the request from Nathan to Me-ma. If there was any doubt about marrying a man she had only known for months, they were gone now. *"How could any woman refuse a guy who had a personality like that?"* she thought to herself as she cradled herself in Nathan's arms.

*

Poker Player had been a busy man since he last talked to Susan. He couldn't shake the thought that there was more to Hanson's death and his trips to the Bureau of Engraving and Printing than what was public. For months he had checked every person who worked at the Bureau of Engraving and Printing. He interviewed anyone who would talk to him and compiled a short list of people who worked there during the Green Paper incident. Each one checked out clean, but one, a Mr. James Cobb, who had moved to Georgia.

Mr. Cobb had retired early from the Federal Government, moved south, instead of back home to Minnesota, and bought a little house outside of Reidsville, Georgia. Poker Player felt that this information should be passed on to Susan and called her in Georgia.

*

It was difficult for Me-ma seeing the sunrise on the day that Susan and Nathan would be departing for D.C. As the sun gently sneaked into her room and its yellowy warmth touched her cheek, she thought of everything that had happened. The last few days had been wonderful, but the events of yesterday were the climax of many dreamy nights for her Susan. Sharing the joy of Susan's proposal, meeting Nathan, and now knowing that her little girl would be in good hands for the future seemed to put a large exclamation on her life. She was satisfied that she had done her part well in raising Susan after her son left her to raise his daughter.

It was seven in the morning and Me-ma wanted to get downstairs to make Susan's favorite breakfast of eggs, ham, grits, and toast. Just then the phone rang.

"Hello?"

"Hello, is Susan Collins there?"

"Yes she is; may I ask who is calling?" Me-ma said with a gentle request and friendly voice.

"Yah, this is, ah, oh, well, Mr. Green!" said Poker Player with a touch of confusion, as he was not prepared to give his name and never told Susan what to call him.

"Mr. Green, I'll call Susan. Just a minute, please!"

Me-ma walked up to Susan's room and knocked on the door gently. "Susan, honey, there is a Mr. Green on the telephone for you."

Susan opened the door and spoke quietly "Mr. Green? I don't know a Mr. Green!"

"Well, dear, it's for you!" Me-ma replied with a come on look!

"Hello, this is Susan Collins! May I help you?"

"Well, hi, little girl, how's everything going? How is Georgia these days?" Poker Player responded with a touch of surprise in his voice.

"Little girl I told you not to call me that! What do you want?"

"Well, litl…, Susan, I have some information for you about the happenings surrounding Senator Hanson's death. Or I think it has something to do with his death!" Poker Player said as he changed his voice from condescending to adult.

"I thought that there was nothing else to it," Susan said, as she shifted her weight from one bare foot to the other and all the while taking in nature's fragrance as it invaded the room. She could hear the annoying voice on the phone but was lost in the beauty before her gaze. Talking to "Mr. Greeeeen" was the last thing she wanted to do!

"You see, James Cobb retired from the Bureau of Printing and Engraving and moved to Reidsville, GA. That's where you are right now!" Poker Player said with a touch of dramatic!

"So?" said Susan, with a, get on with it attitude.

"Well, since you are there right now, why don't you check into him? It may lead to something!"

"OK, I'll think about it," Susan said, but then remembered that only a few people knew where she was.

"Say, how did you know where I was and how did you get this number?"

"I told you before, I can get any number I want! Don't worry about that anyway. Think about checking on James Cobb. OK?" Poker Player was calm, soft, and sort of begging.

"I will think about it, OK? Good bye." was all Susan said as she hung the phone up and walked over to the window. She just wanted to enjoy the golden haze of the sun as it slowly walked its way across the field up to the house on the east.

*

Me-ma obviously was in heaven thinking of her little Susan and marriage. She recalled Susan's mother, Ruth, whom Susan looked exactly like. Ruth was a beautiful woman and on her wedding day she and Darrell Collins made for a picturesque couple. They were right out of a wedding magazine. He, in his black tuxedo and she in white from head... This made Me-ma think, "I wonder if Ruth's wedding veil is still down in the basement? It would be perfect if Susan could wear it on her wedding day!" She called out to Susan! "Susan, come downstairs I want to ask you something."

Susan's countenance as she entered the kitchen seemed to brighten the already sun-lit room. It was apparent that she was in love and not even Mr. Green's call could dampen its effect.

"Yes, Me-ma, what is the question?"

"Well, dear, I was thinking. You know, I've told you many times that you look just like your mother. She was beautiful, graceful, and on her wedding day was exceptionally gorgeous. She wore a beautiful white veil that I still have in a box in the basement. If you like, you can have it and if you think it would be appropriate, wear in on your wedding day. Your mother left her wedding things here because our basement was perfect for storage!" Me-ma said as she led Susan toward the basement step. Then she added! "Why don't you and Nathan go down to the basement and see if you can find it?"

"I think that would be wonderful, Me-ma! From pictures, Mama was beautiful on her wedding day, and I think it would be fantastic wearing her veil." Her excitement was matched by the glow in her eyes.

"Nathan, come down here, I need your help in finding something!" Susan called as she stepped toward the basement door.

Nathan met Susan in the basement as she was pillaging through one box after the other. She told him what they were looking for and why. He thought the idea of her wearing her mother's veil was great. But, which box?

"Boy, your grandmother sure keeps things. There are things here from the eighteen hundreds. She has it all. Even these old and most recent newspapers of the Tattnall Journal are kept for, who knows what? Why?" Nathan queried as he moved one pile to the other side of the room.

As Nathan moved the pile of newspapers one paper fell out and onto the floor. Before Nathan could pick it up, Susan noticed the headlines. It read, "James Cobb - Local resident murdered along the Ohoopee!"

"Wait, Nathan, let me see that paper!" Susan commanded as she reached for the newspaper and almost lost her footing.

"Well, I swanee!" was her amazed exclamation!

"What? Swanee, what does that mean?" Nathan said with a little laugh at her words.

"Oh, swanee is just a Georgian saying! That call I got a few minutes ago was from a man who has been investigating the death of Senator Hanson, who was killed months ago. He has been in touch with me about Hanson's death; he thought my newspaper should know about the strange circumstances of the senator's death. Our investigation didn't lead to much, so we dropped it. But his call was to ask me to check up on this very man, Mr. James Cobb! What do you make of that? And, look at this! It states that his cousin was murdered in France around the same time as his death. There's got to be a connection!" At that very moment, the telephone rang again. Susan, hoping that the call was from Mr. Green, was very willing to talk to him now!

Susan ran up the stairs at break neck speed almost knocking Me-ma down in the process getting to the phone. "Hello, hello, Mr. Green?" Susan stammered with breathlessness.

"Hi, little girl, did you miss my voice?" came the wily voice on the other end of the telephone.

"No, yes, well, I just need to talk" is all Susan could say as she anticipated more information from Mr. Green.

"Did you know that James Cobb was murdered right here in Reidsville along the river? Also, his cousin was murdered in France about the same time." Susan exclaimed as she now was completely brought into the world of Mr. Green.

"Yes, I just found out that very thing, and it doesn't surprise me. That's why I called you back! There has to be a connection, and I would stake my life on the

139

fact that there are those with strong connections and powerful motives who had those two men killed!"

Strong connections? Little did they both know that those with strong connections would literally touch both of their lives!

Saying good bye to Me-ma was difficult for Susan as she found her warmth and understanding made her feel the safest and must welcome of all places on Earth. She knew, however, even though her pending marriage to Nathan made her happier than she had ever been, the mystery of Senator Hanson's death must be first and foremost.

The maglev ride to D.C. was anti-climatic in light of her love for Nathan and their future together. Balancing the excitement of marriage and the investigation of murder drew upon Susan's inner personal power of compartmentalizing things in life. She was totally engrossed with love, but the serious mental make-up of a top notch investigative reporter made it easier for her to stay focused on her job and balance all of the events of present. She could handle it all!

Nathan and Susan arrived back in D.C. and were ready for all the new adventures. Little did they know that what lay ahead would test their faith, test their love, and test their will to proceed with what would be revealed in time.

Chapter

$\approx$12$\approx$

Although the two love birds were consumed with each other it didn't prevent Susan from doing her job. She was in love, but her inner work ethic would not permit her to do anything but a superior job for her newspaper.

Poker Player had contacted Susan more and more and found out that Greely had been killed in France along with a man dressed in a pirate's custom.

Poker Player had checked into the events, but other than what the French newspapers had printed in the Riviera, there was nothing new, only that it was a robbery-murder. He checked with the local French police and their story was the same. But Poker Player wasn't satisfied with their investigation and continued to ask around.

He checked Air France airline records, and, of course, paid small amounts of money for information.

In these records he found the names of twelve people who had flown to the French Riviera. The whereabouts of the twelve could be verified except for one who never took the return trip to the U.S.A. After checking on that person, he found that it was an ex-con named Davis Samplin.

Poker Player gave the information to the French authorities, and they closed the case, assuming that Samplin was on the receiving end of a crooked deal gone wrong. They assumed that he was killed by a partner because there must have been big money involved with the robbery and his partner wanted all the cash.

*

Susan took the information that Poker Player gave her and started to do some snooping around herself. She had shady contacts with people of low character from past dealings to get information. Her contacts were many. They were sorted from high brow to low brow, rich and poor, and some with no morals who would cut a person's throat for a dollar. She used whoever she could as long as they had the right information for a story.

One of her contacts was a shady imp named Demetrius Roston, who seemed to know a lot about everything but never really seemed to know the finer details. He was useful, however, when it came to just having 'some' information about a recent problem or happening. She thought that maybe he would have some little information on the Hanson death. She called the little imp and asked him to meet her. He said he would and they met at the Daily Grill at 1200 18th St. N.W.

Susan got to the restaurant ahead of Demetrius and was enjoying the Daily Grill's ambiance when she noticed a tall man with dark black hair peeking at her from behind his newspaper. The man had come into the grill at the same time as she had and sat across the room in the corner. He glanced at her every now and then, and stopped and read the newspaper.

About that time Demetrius came to her table. Demetrius was very tiny, about four feet five inches, with a small thin mustache that was very straight across his upper lip. He dressed impeccably, and his shoes were shined to the point that he could see himself in them. His voice sounded like what Susan would describe as "impish," but his diction was formal.

"Good day, Ms. Collins how, are you?"

"I'm fine, and you?"

"Well, I'm doing very well, thank you. I have been quite busy with many things and your call interrupted some important matters," he responded with an air of superiority.

"Oh, come on, get off it, Demetrius, I know you aren't doing anything but getting yourself in trouble. You haven't any 'important matters' and you are probably thinking of the next 'Mark' to steal from!"

"I must protest, Ms. Collins! My time is extremely taken up with matters with deep consequences and large sums of money," he pontificated with his head held back and his nose up in the air.

"Yah, sure, now let's get down to some questions. I want to know if you have any information about

Senator Hanson's death?" Susan responded with a flick of her hair and a glance away.

"Well, let's see, Senator Hanson? Wasn't he the gentleman who burned to death when his automobile collided with a gas tanker?"

"Yes, that's him, do you know anything?"

"Now, I'm sure, there would be some monetary compensation for information, correct?" said the imp as he adjusted his seat and leaned forward.

"It all depends on the information and how much," Susan respond with an annoyed look on her face. Then she responded, "Do you have anything?"

"Well, sadly, I don't. The only thing I know is what you probably know, that he was killed by colliding with a gas tanker. But if I get any information I will call you and I'm sure you will compensate me accordingly, right?" as he stood to his feet.

"We'll see about giving you any money based upon your information," Susan said as she remained seated.

"Good day, Ms. Collins, I hope to see you soon." The 'Imp' turned around, adjusted his suit, straightened his body and proudly walked away.

Susan stayed seated, had a cup of coffee and a chicken sandwich, and thought about her next approach to her inquiries.

After her meal, as she was paying the check, she noticed the man in the corner glance at her again. She just glanced back and left.

*
——————— ———————

Nathan had just bought a new car, the 'Aerosphere.' It was one of the latest automobiles on the market. It ran totally on air. Its engine had no internal combustion, and could go for 300 miles before having to be recharged by its onboard compressor. Much of the new forms of transportation were leaning in the direction of air and the technology that came basically from backyard inventors.

Nathan decided to take his new 'wheels' for a ride and test its speed and handling over back roads.

As he departed D. C., he informed the Secret Service that this ride would be without their services, as he would be back in one hour. They were used to these requests and didn't entirely obey but stayed far enough back to gave him room to enjoy life without their visible presence. They did this quite often, and even when he and Susan went to Georgia, they were there just off the property at Me-ma's. Two agents would take turns observing Nathan and staying in Reidsville at a motel.

The air car handled like a fined tuned watch and hugged the road like an expensive sports car. If Nathan hadn't known better, he wouldn't have believed it was propelled by the vapor he breathed.

On his trek he knew of a convenience store that carried his favorite ice swirly. The so-called "Gas Station" was no longer because there was no need for petroleum based products for cars. He decided to stop for the ice swirly.

When he came out of the store, he found a note under a windshield wiper of the car. The note read, "Tell your girlfriend to stop snooping into the Hanson death!" He looked around and saw a black colored car about a block away driving in the opposite direction he would be going and the Secret Service agent's car coming from the other. He got into the Aerosphere and slowly made his way to Susan's.

Arriving at Susan's and insuring the Secret Service agents stayed put, he went to Susan's apartment. She was home and they talked about the note.

"Susan, I'm concerned about your safety. If someone would go to the length this guy did to warn you, there is no telling what he may do." Nathan's concern could be heard in his voice.

"It just proves my suspicions about Hanson's death. It was no accident. Someone killed him to shut his mouth. He must have had some vital information on someone in Washington. Accidental homicide my left foot," Susan was pacing back and forth with her right hand cradling her chin.

"But, Honey, you aren't going to continue with your snooping around, are you?" Nathan stopped her pacing and held her arm.

"Why, yes, I am. You wouldn't want me to stop now would you? If Senator Hanson was murdered, the nation needs to know by whom and why."

"Well, yes, I agree. But I don't want you to get hurt. After all, whoever wrote that note said to stop. If Hanson was murdered, then you could be too," he was concerned and his eyes weren't blinking as he stared at Susan.

"Oh, Nathan, let's not get too dramatic about this, I'm sure I will be OK. I do have you to help me. You will make sure nothing happens to me, won't you," Susan said the words but she too was concerned and wasn't going to let Nathan know it.

The concern for her safety didn't prevent Susan from digging deeper into the mystery and it even caused her to speak to people and frequent places that in her new life with Christ she wouldn't have. As she had told Nathan on the night she turned to the Lord, *"I am not the person you think I am. I have sinned, I have had bad thoughts, done wrong things, gone to the wrong places..."* She wasn't comfortable with the people and places now, but would do so for the sake of the truth.

On one of her night outings without Nathan, she went to a dark and dingy dive named "The Squirrely Dance." It was a so called 'club' and a place now that made her skin crawl. She was amazed how she hadn't seen or understood the dark side of 'The Squirrely Dance' in the past. There was no redeeming value to the place and only offered a fleshy escape for those who didn't know or understand the value of clean living.

When she entered the "club" she went straight to a table were a frequent loser always sat. He was seedy and would do anything to get information on someone in order to blackmail them or sell it to others. He was there, just as if he had never left the place.

"Hi, Dancer," said Susan as she slid into the booth next to the bearded low life. He took the name 'Dancer' from the club he enjoyed.

"Hey, there, 'Porter.' He called her porter because she was a Reporter for the newspaper, and he shortened it and just called her 'Porter.'

"Man, Dancer, it's like you haven't moved from that spot since the last time I saw you here a year ago."

"Yah, I know. I may be in a rut. But I don't mind. I get what I want here. What can I do for you, Porter?"

"Well, Dancer, I'm sure you may recall that Senator who was killed in an auto accident. Senator Hanson was his name."

"Yah, I remember, something about gas and a tanker. That was freaky. Who in the world uses gasoline nowadays?" Dancer nonchalantly replied.

"Yes, that's him. He hit that gas tanker; it exploded and caught the car on fire. He died at the scene. Did you ever hear of anything shady about that situation?" Susan asked as she leaned forward trying to draw Dancer's attention to the seriousness of her inquiry.

"Nope, haven't heard anything on the streets."

"Are you sure? There may be some money in it if you have any information." Susan's questioning Dancer's knowledge was only a formality in this conversation. She knew Dancer enough to know that he wouldn't lie and that he didn't have the information she needed.

"I'm sure, Porter. I got nothin," said Dancer as he lifted his drink and smiled.

"Thanks, Dancer. I knew that if anyone would have something, you would. See-ya later."

"See-ya Porter. Keep your ink wet," Dancer said as Susan got up and left the table.

———————— * ————————

The next day
*
———————— ————————

Nathan was sitting in his room at the Residency flipping through a magazine when his cell phone rang.

"Hello."

"I'm telling you to stop that girl of yours from snooping around. Do you hear me," said an obviously disguised voice.

"Hey. Who is this? What do you mean? Why?" Nathan responded with a sense of concern.

"She's gonna get herself in trouble with all of her questions, and I won't be responsible," the voice was raised now and quickly demanding. "I won't warn you or her again. Do you understand?" With that the caller hung up and the phone went silent.

Nathan called Susan and told her of the call and the dangers of her continuing on. He suggested that they let the Secret Service in on the warnings. He tried to convince her that it was for her own safety but she wouldn't have anything to do with his concerns.

"Nathan, I know I am onto something here, and if I quit now, we may never find out what really happened to Hanson," Susan said with an imploring tone.

"But, Susan, I love you too much to see anything bad happen to you."

"I know, sweetheart. But for some reason I just feel like I'm not in danger even in spite of the warnings. I tell'ya what, let's give it one more week, and if I don't find anything out, I will let it go. Is that OK with you?"

"Well, OK. But I don't really like it. But I know you will continue anyway. So, we'll give it one week," Nathan gave in but with reservations.

*

The next night

*

Susan had one more "sack" of information, as she called her sources, and it was a pawn shop owner by the name of Tonya Relavan. Tonya was one of the few female pawnbrokers and had the heart of a tiger. Everyone knew her to be honest, straight forward, and fair. She came across like a princess but was as tough as a king protecting his turf.

Susan got to Tonya's shop around 7 PM. It was dark, and the streets in that area were dimly lit.

When Susan entered the shop, Tonya greeted her with her familiar sing song voice of "Hi'ya sweety. What'ya up to!"

"Hey, Tonya. How's business been?"

"Not bad. I could always use some more money. But can't complain. What can I do fir'ya?" Tonya met Susan around the counter and in front of the caged area.

"Well, Tonya, I'm out sniffing out bad dirt on what I think is a murder; the death of Senator Hanson a few months ago. You know anything about it?" Susan asked as she touched Tonya's arm and smoothed her hand over her obviously silk shirt.

"Hanson? No. Haven't heard nothin," Tonya replied as she looked down on Susan's hand and smiled in recognition of Susan admiring her shirt.

"I was afraid of that. It seems like no one has anything on the subject. Maybe I'm just barking up a tree that has nothin in it."

"Well, dear, if I hear anything I'll let ya know," Tonya slowly moved around to the other side of the counter and back behind the caged bars.

150

"OK Tonya. See ya," Susan went to her car and decided to go home.

By the time Susan arrived at home, it was around 8:30, and she just wanted to relax with some TV watching and a bowl of cornflakes.

After she unlocked the door to her apartment and entered, someone grabbed her from behind. Whoever it was was very strong as she couldn't move nor remove his hand from her mouth.

"Don't move, and be quiet," said this gruff voice, but with a touch of familiarity.

"Who are you?" asked Susan without resisting.

"Never mind who I am. I want you to stop digging into the Hanson death. It can only lead to your harm."

"But I'm just trying to get a story for my newspaper. That's my job," she said as if that would really make a difference to someone who could probably kill her right then and there.

"You don't know what you are getting into, and how much it can hurt you in many ways."

"What will happen to me if I don't?" she said with an air of confidence and bravado.

"Well, for one, you could stop breathing, and for the other, that boyfriend of yours could get hurt. Do you understand me?"

"Yes. I do understand. I promise I will take another approach," is all she said.

"I'm not sure I know what that means. But you have been warned. Stop or else," replied the menacing invader.

"Yes. I will. I will," was Susan's come back to what she took as a not too threatening voice.

Her captor somewhat loosened his grip on her body but didn't completely let go and said, "Suco stop the snooping around"! He then pushed her to the floor, turned, and ran out of the door.

Susan's mind went numb, not by the push to the floor but by that name 'Suco,' that's the name Me-ma had called her, and no one else.

She picked herself up from the floor and ran out the door after the invader, all the while shouting, "Why did you call me Suco? Who are you?"

Just as she got out the door she heard gun shots, and a familiar voice shouting "Put it down!"

"Bam! Bam! Bam!"

When she reached the hall, she saw a man standing at the right of her door with a gun, which obviously had been fired, and the invader running down the hall on the left. He was limping and blood was making a trail on the paisley carpet.

The injured intruder was too fast for Susan and the stranger who had fired the gun, and he got quickly down the stairway and out of the building and into the night.

As Susan stood there with the stranger, and after gaining her composure asked him, "Who are you?"

He turned to her and said, "Well, little girl," with a large grin on his face.

"You. You. Well, finally," is all that came out of her mouth.

"I'm sorry we have to meet like this but it couldn't have happened at a better time, I'd say," said her hero.

"I would say so, Mr. Green. Say do you always shoot people who aren't shooting at you?" said Susan as she put her arms around his left arm and directed him to her apartment.

"No, but that guy had a gun. When I saw him run from your apartment and you shouting after him, I thought that maybe you had been hurt. Beside, he pointed it at me," as he patted her hand and gave her a concerned look.

"A gun. I didn't know," as she looked back with her wide dark eyes.

Susan ushered Mr. Green or as he was known by the Vice President, 'Poker Player,' into the apartment and had him sit on the couch, and just stared at him.

"Well, is that all you're going to do is stare? Say something," Poker Player pleaded.

"I don't know what to say. You said I would never meet you. Now here you are at the very time I needed someone. Why now?" she gushed out.

"Well, little gir…Susan, sorry, I felt it was time I talked to you in person. There is no sense being secretive anymore. I just decided to come here tonight. Lucky I did," as he smiled.

"I would say so. Lucky isn't the word though. I'd say providence."

"Well, whatever. I'm here, and how do you do?" he said with his hand outstretched.

She took his hand, shook it, and said, "I'm doing well, now, thank you," with the same wide eyed response.

"Who was that guy and what did he want?" Poker asked with a look of 'let's get to the bottom of this.'

"I don't know but I'm sure curious. He grabbed me when I came in tonight. I don't know how he got in, but I don't think he really wanted to harm me. I think he meant just to warn me."

"How do you know that it was just a warning?" he asked as he looked around the room.

"It was his mannerisms and body language. He just didn't come across like he wanted to harm me. I felt like he wanted to protect me more than anything," at that moment she and Poker Play noticed an open window across the room and pointed. "That's how he got in," she confirmed for the both of them.

"Do you have any information on Hanson's death?" he asked with a look of 'I hope so.'

"Nope. Nothing. Everything I have tried comes up negative," Susan confessed with a shrug of her shoulders.

"In any case I would be careful, and make sure you lock your doors all the time," he said as he stood to his feet.

"I'll be cautious. Where you going?"

"Well, I don't think he will be back. I think you are safe. Do you want me to stay?" Poker Player asked as he moved closer to the door.

"No. I'll be fine. I'll let you know if I come up with something. Hey, by the way, thanks for being my hero tonight," she said as she reached over and kissed his cheek.

"Well, that was worth it," he stated as he patted the spot of the kiss.

"Oh, how do I get in contact with you?" Susan asked as he was departing.

"Same deal as before. I'll get in contact with you. See ya," he was gone and she shut and locked the door.

After Poker Player left, Susan locked the window the intruder came through, and thought about calling Nathan but decided not to. She knew Nathan would be concerned and would want to come over, along with his government protectors. Because she was afraid that they would find something out, she decided to tell Nathan in person later.

*

It was late on the second day after Susan was attacked in her apartment. She, however, didn't think of it as being an attack as the guy just seemed to want to talk and warn. All through the ordeal, she had not felt threatened for some reason.

Her phone rang around 6 PM just after she arrived from the office.

"Hello."

"Hello. Is Susan Collins there?" said a calm distinct voice.

"Yes. This is she."

"Ms. Collins, I have some information about Suco for you," the voice calmly declared.

"Suco? How do you know that name? Who is this?" Susan raised her voice and demanded.

"That's all I can say. If you want to talk about Suco, come to 1347 North Barcross Street now, and make sure you are alone. Do not bring your boyfriend either," demanded the calm distinct voice.

"Say. I don't know who are. I don't know what may be waiting for me there. Why can't I bring Nathan?" Susan asked and kind'a knew she wouldn't get an affirmative reply to anything.

"Trust me. You are not in danger. You will get the answers to many questions. And you will know about Suco," calmly responded the lady.

"There is only one person who knows that name. I want to know who else knows it," Susan herself calm now replied but in the back of her mind thinking, *'I hope I don't regret doing this.'* "I will be there in about 30 minutes."

"Fine. See you then." Click.

While driving to Barcross Street Susan's mind was running crazy. She was only called 'Suco' by Me-ma and couldn't figure out how anyone else could know that name.

When she arrived at 1347 North Barcross, she didn't immediately get out of her car but just sat there and surveyed the surroundings. The neighborhood was clean, and had well groomed lawns. It was probably upper middle class but nothing ostentatious. The house was a small white one story building with a black Mercedes in the driveway. The Mercedes was the latest fuel cell model; it got 53 MPG and was probably the safest car on the road.

As she slowly got out of her car, she thought, *'Whoever lives here isn't hurting and probably can't be too dangerous.'* The thought helped calm her down.

After ringing the door bell, she reminded herself to stay clam, remember that she was a reporter, and even though she was personally involved here, she must get the story and be as unbiased as possible.

As the door opened she noticed a small brass name plate on it that had the name Humbolt. The door was opened by a tall woman, probably in her late forties; she was dressed in a Nurses uniform and had reddish hair. She smiled nicely at Susan. "Please come in, Ms. Collins," was her warm greeting.

"Would you care for a drink? I can offer you just about anything," was the obviously handsome woman's disarming welcome.

"Nothing, thank you," Susan said as she glanced around trying to see anything that may give her a clue of why she was there.

"Well, Ms. Collins. I know you are curious as to what is going on. Please understand that you are safe here and there is someone who wants to see you. I will take you to him in a minute," said the tall host but not giving anything away too quickly.

"Please, tell me who you are?" Susan asked.

"I will let him tell you who I am if he wishes. But first, please don't be alarmed when you see him as he has been hurt, and looks pretty rough."

"Who? Who is hurt?" Susan's concern and curiosity was growing.

"Please come with me. Remember he is hurt."

"OK. I'm calm," Susan responded with a little bit of annoyance.

She was ushered into a bedroom that looked more like a hospital room than a bedroom. There was a bed against the outside wall with its headboard facing into the room. A dim florescent fixture affixed to the wall gave light to the person in the bed but not his face. The form in the bed lay motionless as Susan approached.

"Hi," said a gentle but weak voice.

"Hello," is all Susan said, not because she was fearful, but because she was numbed by the intrigue of the situation.

"I have been waiting for many years to see you this close," said her bed welcoming host.

"For many years? How do you know me? Who are you?" Susan's voice cracked and as she moved closer to get a look at his face.

He responded, "Suco."

"How do you know that name?"

"I gave it to you!" his voice was weaker and she could tell that it had a touch of emotion.

"You gave it to me? My grandmother gave me that name when I was a baby!" Her comeback to his declaration came with force and correction.

"No. I gave it to you as a play on your name Susan Collins – Su-co. You had just been born and I held you in my arms. Mother liked the nickname and it stuck," he was obviously holding back great emotion.

"My mother. Did you know her?"

"I don't mean your mother. I meant my mother."

Susan stood silent, her mind was in a fog; it was muddied by many events that had led to this moment.

"Suco," said the weak voice.

Susan came out of the fog, and stepped closer in order to see his face. She saw a roughed face man, probably in his late forties or early fifties, with jet black hair, and bright blue bloodshot eyes, and it was the man who had broken into her apartment. She slowly reached her hand out.

He said again, "Suco."

"Daddy," she said as she slowly squeezed his hand.

"Yes. I am," was his gentle weak reply.

"Daddy?"

"Yes!"

"Daddy. I thought I would never meet you," she exclaimed with a very nervous smile.

"I know, sweetheart, I know," he said as his hand shook and his voice cracked. "I'm so sorry I didn't stay and raise you."

"Oh, Daddy. Where have you been. Why did you leave me?"

"I was wrong. I was wrong and selfish," he said as he squeezed her hand. "I was weak and was only thinking of myself."

"Daddy, why now? Why did you break into my apartment? Why didn't you reveal yourself before?" she asked with rapid questioning.

"I know you have many questions. I promise I will answer them all. But I don't have a lot of time. I hurt bad and I don't think I'm gon'a make it," as he spoke he began to cough and spit up blood.

The woman standing at the door came closer and helped calm his chest and head as he coughed. She swabbed his forehead with a damp cloth and cleaned the blood from his lips.

"Who are you?" asked Susan looking at the woman.

"Susan, this is Dana Humbolt. She's a very close friend and an emergency room nurse. We have known each other for years. She is helping until..." his words trailed off as he coughed again and pushed back on the bed.

"Until. Until what?" Susan demanded.

"Ms. Collins, your father isn't going to make it. He was shot in the spleen at your apartment and there is no fix outside of an operating room, and he won't let me take him to one," the nurse friend said with what was obviously tender concern.

"Oh Daddy. Why didn't you explain last night. This wouldn't have happened then. You wouldn't have been shot."

"I know. It's just another one of my mistakes. I have been so foolish for some many years. But it's too late now," he said as he longingly looked into her eyes. It was as if he was seeing for the first time and couldn't get enough of it.

"Daddy, tell me everything."

"I will. Dana, would you please excuse us for awhile?" As Dana left the room, he coughed and she turned and mouthed to Susan, *"Please make it quick!"* Susan nodded, 'OK.'

Susan and her father spoke for an hour and half. In between their conversation he coughed, spit up blood, and cried. She cried, wiped tears from her eyes, and gingerly hugged her father when she could. Many times she would stop from talking and just lay her face against his cheek and pat it.

In that hour and a half he told her everything about his life that he could or dared. His life wasn't pretty and he told only those things that mattered to her life and her snooping into the death of Senator Hanson.

"Suco, it was hard leaving you to be raised by my mother. I didn't care about anything after your mother died and just gave up on life. I knew I couldn't be a good father to you and wasn't willing to even try. I'm sorry," his explanations were confused at time, but that is all he had.

Susan listened and tried to understand, but there were questions that couldn't really be answered in such a short time. She was more concerned about getting him to the hospital than listening to life's remorses right now.

Her father was adamant about not going to the hospital because it would bring up more questions about how, why and who. He just felt that it would be better to let things be as they were. For him it was enough that he got to talk to and touch his daughter after all these years.

He told how he had traveled around the country just doing whatever he could to make ends meet. He had gone back to see Susan a few times before she reached two years of age but quit going when he and the bottle became close friends.

For a short time, his mother had known where he was and had talked to him over the telephone a few times but then he just dropped from sight and sound. Rose never learned where he was after that and continued to raise and love Susan on her own. Darrell did keep track of his daughter at a distance but never let her see him.

When Susan moved to Washington D.C., Darrell followed there and checked her life through the newspaper articles she wrote and occasionally followed her. He would even walk right by her on the street, but she didn't have a clue he was there.

While in D.C., he became acquainted with the darker side of life and began to meet gangsters that had friends in the government. At first he was a small time hood, but soon worked his way up to white collar crime and the social elite crowd, and then on to killing for hire. He met Senator Hanson through Greely who was one of those so called social elite criminals. It was Senator Hanson who introduced Darrell to the President.

The President asked Senator Hanson to get him Darrell Collins because he had some very important things for him to do.

Hanson, and very few individuals in the world knew about a secret passage that led to the While House from a concealed stone shack off of Pennsylvania Ave and W. Executive Ave N.W.. The shack was locked but never really watched by the Secret Service because it was thought to be of no real value. It looked like the other historic stone structures that surrounded the area.

However, for a person who was in the know, had the right key, and correct directions, the secret passage from the stone shack became a clandestine entrance to the White House and a small room in its basement.

The secret small room was the place that the President met Collins to discuss Hanson's death, Greely and his cousin's death, and the one pirate, Davis Samplin, who was killed on the Riviera. Darrell Collins was the only survivor of all those killings because he was the killer.

"Sweetheart, it's time for me to go. I don't have much time left. We must move now," her father told Susan after the hour and a half.

"I'm gon'a let my body be found by the authorities, and it must look like a robbery gone bad."

His plan was to get in his car and drive to a seedy part of town and just die; His gunshot wounds would be taken as a robbery gone wrong resulting in his death at the scene. It was a good plan and would eliminate any questions for his daughter to explain.

Susan was a total wreck with her father's plan. She now knew her father and wasn't going to let him go. Her begging and pleading were to no avail, however, and, finally, she gave in and was willing to let him go.

Dana and Susan helped dress Darrell with the same clothes he had had on when he was shot at Susan's apartment. His plan was to make sure that there would be no questions about his death. He was to be a man killed in a robbery and that was that.

As Darrell was helped into the driver's seat, Susan, crying all the while, kept kissing, and hugging her father. The madness of the moment made her numb and insensitive to common sense and demanded a reality of its own that screamed "get it done"!

"Daddy, I love you. I will never forget you. I'm sorry that your life wasn't good," she then remembered Jesus. "Daddy, I want to see you again. Jesus can help you. He will forgive you," was her last ditch effort to hang on, even at this last moment.

"Sweety, I must go. I don't think I can hold on much longer."

"Daddy, if you repent and give your life to Jesus, you can be saved, and I will see you again," was her feeble try to hang on.

"My lovely, Sucu, it's too late for me. I can't, I won't, I must go," was his only reply to her spiritual band aid to a life that was deeper into darkness than she could imagine.

"No, Daddy. No. Please, Daddy," she pleaded as Dana held her arms and pulled her away from her father's side.

"Please, Dana, let me give him one more kiss, please," Dana released her grip and Susan fell into her father's arms, and they kissed one last time. He then pushed her away, closed the door and drove away.

Dana and Susan, both crying the whole time, followed Darrell to the spot he had picked out earlier. After he stopped and parked, they just drove on by and back to her father's house.

Through sobs and heart rendering cries Susan would try to have a conversation with Dana about the why's and reasons but no answer would console her.

Dana really didn't know too much about Darrell's life of crime and especially about his killings. She knew enough to know that he was involved in crime but never pressed him on how deep. They had met in a bar years ago and had become friends. It was enough for her that Darrell could be counted on to hear her inner hurts when she needed someone to vent on.

Most of the answers Susan received from Dana were of a general nature and about her and Darrell's relationship, which was just a friendship and nothing else.

"Although I hate what we just did and what he is doing, I know it is probably for the best," Dana shared with Susan.

"How can this be the best?" Susan responded with a sniffle.

"Well, what he told you is probably more than what I know. What I do know is that he is involved with crime and wants to keep you from having to explain his life to the authorities. It is his way of protecting you." Dana's explanation was her best attempt to strengthen her resolve and to ease her own pain.

"Yes, from what he told me, his life was or is, a mess and there would be a lot of explaining."

They arrived at Dana's house and sat in the living room and talked. Susan asked Dana to just tell her everything she could about her dad and the man she only knew by the name "Daddy."

Dana shared about how she and Darrell had met, the many hours talking over Dana's hurts and relationships, and time spent laughing and the occasional meals.

Susan was learning through Dana about a man who was a mystery, a father with a personality somewhat like hers, and dark stranger who would remain in the shadow of her heart and mind.

They spoke until the sun came up, and during the long hours of the night, they went through Darrell's few photos and private things he had brought to Dana's house although it really didn't reveal much of their man of mystery. Susan did take the wallet photo of her father, however, and Susan and Dana became friends through this strange meeting.

---------- * ----------

After leaving Dana's house, Susan drove to the area where Darrell had parked, but the car was gone. She stopped her car and cried for about thirty minutes and drove home.

Upon arriving home, she found a police squad car just arriving at her apartment complex. She knew why they were there and slowly made her way to the front of the building pretending to be just coming home.

"Excuse me, are you Ms. Susan Collins?" asked a chubby police officer and his partner as she approached the door.

"Yes."

"May we speak to you for a moment, please," the officer gently said.

"What about? Have I broken a law?" Susan said as calmly as possible.

"Could we speak in your apartment please? It would be better," the taller of the two officers asked as they walked towards the door of the building.

"Sure. Follow me."

After they all entered Susan's apartment the officers asked Susan to sit down as the news they had would come hard.

"OK. I'm seated, what's up?" she said but knowing what was coming.

"Is your father's name Darrell Collins?"

"Yes. That's his name, but I haven't seen him since I was a baby. He left shortly after I was born, and I never knew him," was her reply, and it came with great effort.

"We are sorry to inform you that a Darrell Collins was found dead last night. We think he was killed while someone was robbing him. His body was found in his car, and he had been shot."

"What? How do you know it's my father?"

"He had your name, address, and phone number in his wallet. Also in his wallet was a piece of paper with the name Rose Collins in Georgia. Who is Rose Collins?"

"Rose is my grandmother and his mother."

"Would you like for us to notify his mother?"

"Oh, no. I will do it!"

"We are so very sorry for your loss. But we will need for you to come down to the morgue to identify the body. Could you come with us now," the gentler of the two officers requested.

"Yes. I'll come now, but I have only seen him in pictures, I wouldn't know him on sight," as she broke down and began to sob and the officers tried to console her.

Susan identified the body the best she could, or at least that's what she told the police, and was driven back to her apartment. She was told that her grandmother must come and identify the body also since Susan could not positively identify it. She was also told that the police were looking for his killer or killers, but it didn't look good as most of those kinds of crimes just go unsolved.

*

The next day Susan called Me-ma and told her about Darrell. Me-ma cried and told her that she would take the next flight out of Savannah and be there as soon as possible.

Susan lied to her grandmother and didn't tell her the circumstance of her father's life, but just that he had gotten in contact with her, and they had started to have a father and daughter relationship. She told Me-ma the robbery killing story and left it at that.

Me-ma identified Darrell's body, and it was released to them for burial. She had the body sent back to Reidsville, Georgia, for burial in the city cemetery. Me-ma and Susan went back to attend the funeral, which was held two days later, and grieve with the few relatives who knew Darrell.

Susan didn't tell Nathan about her father, his death or any of the circumstances surrounding the whole mess. In her confusion, she felt it best that Nathan not know until the appropriate time. She didn't quite know how to inform him that his own father was a crook and had hired murderers.

When it came time for her to leave and go to Reidsville for the funeral, she told Nathan she had to go out of town on newspaper business and that she would be back in a few days. Nathan knew nothing of Darrell Collins or his father's associations. Susan would leave it for another time.

Chapter

≈13≈

Once again Jack found himself sitting quietly in his office staring out the window, but looking at nothing in particular. His body was in the most powerful chair in the world, but his mind was floating here and there amongst dark dealings, spiritual wooing, and emotional beckoning that seemed to be real, but often transparent and with a hint of foreboding.

It seemed lately that every time he would get alone and let himself think of the future his mind would see his son. It was strange, but nothing seemed to have the importance as a conversation with Nathan as he had had with him in the swimming pool.

He couldn't figure out why he felt so discontent. After all, the Green Paper deal was completed. He had more money than he knew what to do with. The loose ends had been taken care of with the killing of Cobb and his cousin.   Only one other person knew of his murderous connections. His affair with Lora was just what he wanted and Nora was told the truth. But, still he felt confused and in need!

*

Albert had just finished repairing a leaky sink in the main kitchen and was on his way back to his cubbyhole when he had the overpowering urge to pray. This wasn't just the urge to pray and speak with God, but a desperate time to intercede. He had had these special urges before and knew not to shrug them off, but with this one he felt like others were to intercede as well. He called home and asked Delores to pray also. He also decided to seek out Wannetta Morales.

As Albert settled into his usual praying place amongst the tools and other instruments of his trade, he had this sense that a war was about to begin. The comfortable walls surrounding this man took on the appearance of a war room with soldiers stationed against intruders of all sorts. However, the soldiers protecting Albert could not be seen by the human eye unless they were in tune with heaven and the important matter at hand. Albert was unaware of their presence, but very much aware of the commission that was put upon him at this hour.

If Albert had opened his eyes, he would not have recognized his little cubbyhole and plumbing tools. The walls looked like they had been turned to glass, not completely clear, but glistened like gold with just a touch of royal blue. The floor seemed to float with each cry of intercession from Albert and whenever he would shout with authority-which only comes from someone who knows their mission - it would shimmer with traces of precious gems.

Albert would find himself becoming rigid every now and then and felt like hands were supporting his effort of prayer. Although he knew he was alone in that room, he also knew that Delores and Wannetta were praying as well; *it must be their faith and prayers he felt.* He was right in the prayers of Delores and Wannetta, but there was a heavenly being praying with him. The Holy Spirit was interceding for the saints and orchestrating this opera of eternal music that would change lives.

A life was in the balance between light and dark. No mere passive prayer would make unmovable wills give way to truth and right thinking. Albert's intercession, coupled with his earthly partners in prayer and the unction of the Spirit and faith, would be the only power capable of making a mind open for truth.

Just when Albert felt like he was reaching a point of accomplishment, he would be gripped by darkness that was tangible in nature and he knew he was feeling what Jack Prinston felt. The darkness was horrible. It permeated every pore and engulfed every thought, captivating one's eyes and making it impossible to see past the immediate abyss of night.

Just when Albert felt like giving up and quitting, there was a whoosh of feather-like movement and everything would become light again with renewed power, vigor, and faith. He grasped the new found strength to continue on and proceed to the next encounter. It was at that moment he realized that this intercession must be accompanied with rebuke of those forces that were directing Jack Prinston into eternal hell.

"In the name that is above every name, the name of Jesus, the King of Kings and Lord of Lords, the all powerful Son of Man and Son of God, I rebuke you demons of darkness and rulers over men of power! I stand between you and Jack Prinston. You will give him room to think, to respond, and to accept with full conscience his fate. You will stand back in order for him to hear and make his own decision! Now be gone!" At that Albert fell to the floor with a moan and a sense that the intercession had accomplished God's desired results. Jack Prinston was now in a place without any outside interference to hear, accept or reject, and to fully determine his destiny. Would he receive the truth?

*

Nathan went to his room in the White House residence to think about the past weekend and his future with Susan. He knew that he must seek God about what to do and how he should proceed with Susan and knelt by his bed to inquire of his sovereign. Although the topic was to be Susan and his marriage he found himself blocked every time he mentioned it. God was directing elsewhere and Nathan had to respond.

Nathan had prayed often since his conversion and usually found no interference when he knelt before his Lord, but this time he felt dark forces fighting his conversation. Intercession was new to Nathan, but he dove in with the abandonment of youth, but the sure confidence of a son of God.

His voice rose to pray for Susan and out of his mouth came "Jack Prinston, hear the message, receive the truth, repent and be saved. Now is the time for salvation!" He was praying for his father! A little confused, but knowing that a special thing was happening, Nathan preceded with little effort and confidence that God was in charge.

As he prayed, an excitement grew within him and his prayers of intercession became forceful with a touch of 'right now' importance. He couldn't wait to see his father as he felt that God was going to use him to lead his dad to God!

*

It was strange for Jack to be thinking about his needs, but he found himself walking out of his office, ignoring Jane and going down the stairway to the basement and Albert Frank's cubbyhole. He was drawn to the memory of Albert the night the water pipes broke in the China Room. For some reason Jack had this inner pull that lit his path to the one person who might give him some answers. Nathan might have been the opening source of light, but Albert was to be the man that God was directing him to.

*

Albert had just stood to his feet after his time of intercession for the President when he walked in.

Albert was surprised, to say the least, but considering what had just happened in prayer, it made sense.

Jack looked somewhat confused, but stood at the door entrance and just stared at Albert. He was blinking his eyes, lifting his hands in a questioning manner, and had a questioning look upon his face. Albert knew that God had set the stage for a life and death confrontation with Jack Prinston.

"Excuse me, Mr. Frank, may I speak with you?" Jack asked with a please don't refuse me look. "I need to speak to someone who has your kind of knowledge."

"My kind of knowledge, Mr. President?" replied Albert, knowing that it couldn't be about plumbing or other material repairs. "Do you need help with some plumbing, sir?"

"No, sir, Mr. Frank, I need help with something that goes way beyond plumbing or repairs. But maybe it is a repair of the human mind!" Jack still looked confused, but had made his mind up that he would get some answers.

"Please, Mr. President, call me Albert if you wish." Albert walked over to Jack and motioned for him to sit down in the old recliner that had been there since the cubbyhole had been redecorated upon his arrival as Plumber's Helper.

"Mr. President, you look like a man that has a lot on his mind. Is there anything I can do for you?" Albert slowly took the rickety chair that was to have been repaired months ago, but never came under the expert hands of the craftsman because of other commitments.

"Albert, I do have a lot on my mind, but I just can't shake this inner fear I have of eternity. I know it sounds weird and funny, but I feel like I have a clear head and an open passage way for proper thinking. It is like I have just come out of a coma and am hearing things correctly now. I hope you won't brush these comments off and think that I have just had too many pressures on me, as I am the President. It goes way past being the President; I am a human first and then the President, if that makes sense."

"Sir," said Albert, "I think I know why you are here. God has set this time up and considers it a divine appointment for you."

"Yes, Albert, that's it, a divine appointment. It feels just like the time I was talking with Nathan, my son, in the swimming pool. He too spoke like it was a divine appointment. I can understand that!" Jack leaned toward Albert and placed his hand on his arm.

"Albert, there are things I have done that could ruin many people; things that are not pretty, and things that could make people go to jail. My life in general has been made up of many mistakes, perpetuated by more mistakes, compounded by pride, hate, and avarice. The only thing I really know right now, however, is that I must talk with someone about them. You came to mind because I have heard of your solid life and overheard you speak to others about truth; which is something I try to steer clear of, but now seem to need more than anything." Jack's confusion seemed to fall away as he talked.

"Well, sir, if what you say about your life, confusion, and wanting truth is true, then you are on the road to a new beginning."

"What do you mean, a new beginning, Albert? How can a person have a new beginning? You just don't know the terrible things in my life!" This confession from the President of the United States, in that setting, with a lowly plumber must have been one for the books. Who in their wildest dreams would have thought that such a powerful person would have opened himself up with such abandonment?

"Mr. President..."

"Please call me Jack!" stated the President.

"Well, Jack, I know of your talk with Nathan in the swimming pool. He shared it with me. We have been praying for you for some time now. In fact, there are many people praying for you! However, as important as their prayers are for you, you are the only person who can really make the difference in your life. If you will submit to the ultimate truth of the universe you will realize truth." Jack could see Albert's serious expression, but gentle look that made it easy for him to receive what he was hearing.

"When it all boils down to its lowest denominator, it really doesn't matter what you have done that is bad. It only matters what you do with the one maximum question in life. And that is 'What have you done with Jesus?'" All at once every noise making piece of equipment, the ambient sounds of the building, and the quiet inhale and exhale of their lungs were drowned out by the magnitude of the question just asked by the plumber-preacher.

"What have I done with Jesus?" asked Jack. "What do you mean? I have never done anything with him! Matter of fact, I never gave him a moment's thought." He caught himself and then went on. "Well, I thought about him after Nathan and I had the talk in the pool. But, as a whole, I haven't done much with him! What must I do?"

"Well, Jack, you have already stated you are a sinner, by the very confession of your wrongs. Do you realize that God doesn't approve of those things and has a right to condemn you for them?" Albert looked directly into Jack's eyes that did not turn away or flinch for the question.

"Yes, Albert, I do!" was all Jack said.

"Ok; do you think you could ever make things right with God over those sins? Do you think you would be a good sacrifice to correct all the wrongs, since you are so tainted by darkness and sin? Do you think there must be another way to appease God for your sins?" The seriousness of the questions were going deep into Jack's soul and he felt like a hot poker was touching each secret of damnation and taking residency. It was unbearable for such a one time confident man!

"Man, if that's what it takes to be right with God, I am lost forever. What can I do to get free from this guilt and constant darkness of mind?" If it hadn't been for Albert keeping his hand upon Jack, he probably would have been on his knees in front of Albert.

"Well, Jack, I'm sure Nathan told you about Jesus and why He came to die on the cross. Jesus was the perfect sacrifice that you could not be. He took all of those wrong-doings, the sin, the darkness, and the many mistakes upon himself in order for us to be right with God through His intervention and appeasement. He was sinless, but took on our sin in order for us to be acceptable to God the Father, and able to be free from sin's punishment in hell."

By now, Jack had some small tears slowly making their way down his nose, dripping on his chin and into his mouth. It was obvious that the message of truth was cooling the hot poker in his soul.

"Albert, I don't completely understand, but I do believe what you just said. What must I do?" Jack now was on his knees in front of Albert, with his head down and ready for anything.

"Jack, just confess your sins to God. Cry out to him for your life, acknowledge Jesus as the one who took your punishment and then make your mind up that you will live for and walk with Him! Can you do that, Jack?" Albert forcefully asked as he pressed firmly upon Jack's shoulder.

Just as Jack began to reply, the lights flickered, the basement equipment seemed to make more noise, and the basement began to smell like something was dead or dying. It was obvious that dark forces were at work trying to disrupt, dissuade, or at the least side track what was taking place.

Jack was about to comment upon the basement happenings, but Albert pressed the point about repentance, saying, "Don't mind those things in this room, just press into how you feel and the importance of getting right with God. The things that are happening in this room right now are not of God, but of the Devil trying to keep you from making the right eternal decision."

Jack nodded his head in the affirmative and lowered it again and cried out to God. Albert quietly prayed and stood in the gap for Jack, knowing that dark demons would try anything to keep Jack from proceeding forward now.

Albert didn't listen in as Jack confessed dirty deeds, murderous events, and other forms of sin that are common to all humans. It was enough for him to know that Jack Prinston was meeting God through Christ and coming face to face with his life and what forgiveness is all about.

Jack's time of repentance and emotional release went on for about two hours. Many in the White House were looking for the President, but had no idea that he would be in the basement having a personal meeting with the universal President of creation.

*

Nathan ran out of his room and down the stairs from the private residence and made his way to his father's office. He wanted to talk to his father, to see if now was the time for God to use him to lead him to Christ, but was stopped dead in his tracks when he reached Jane Dean's office door. For some unknown reason he felt that all with his father was right. The urgency of talking to Dad did not seem to be important right now. He would wait.

*

As Jack was getting up from his knees, with what was obviously a new countenance, one which radiated peace, joy, and forgiveness, he grabbed Albert and gave him a hug. Rightly so that this was an appropriate time for hugs, but with the President of the United States, it felt a little uncomfortable to Albert. Nevertheless, Albert reciprocated and threw his arms around the President and both cried in each other's arms.

As Jack was wiping the tears away, he said to Albert, "I would appreciate it if you would tell no one of this meeting or what has happened. It isn't that I don't want to tell anyone, but there are things I must do before I am ready to divulge my faith in Christ right now. I hope you understand?"

Albert was not taken back by this request and said, "Yes, Mr. President, I do, and I will tell no one until you permit me. It will be hard to keep it quiet for too long, as there always is evidence of a new birth in Christ. People will ask you questions, I'm sure. Nathan will be one of them."

"So, we are back to Mr. President again?" Jack said with a wink toward Albert.

"Yes, sir. We may be brothers in Christ now, but you are still the President and your office deserves that respect. However, is there anything I can do for you in your new found life?"

"Not right now Albert, but I'm sure I will need your expertise in the near future, both plumbing and spiritual!" At that Jack walked away from Albert, the celestial cubbyhole, and into a world that he must face with his new found purity. The President had just become a good man!

---- * ----

August 1st:

---- * ----

Nathan and Susan had set the date for their marriage for the end of September. They had informed Me-ma, Nathan's parents, and made all the arrangements that were necessary. Everyone was happy and looking forward to Nathan and Susan's wedding, which would be held in the State Dinning room.

*

Everyone associated with the President could sense that something was different about him. Although they couldn't put their finger on it, they knew from his quieter demeanor and "take time with you" style.

Nathan didn't press his dad with any questions, as he just knew that something had taken place and didn't want to ruin what God may have accomplished. Albert did tell Nathan just to be patient and he would see some great things. Nora found Jack to be more attentive, but she was guarded as Jack could be a coy deceiver and she didn't want to be on the receiving end of some lover's ploy that had nothing to do with her. Jane tried to make advances toward Jack, but found he brushed her off with an understanding acceptance that was confusing to her and made her more persistent to confront him later. Lora was informed that the President would be tied up with very important matters for some time and that he would call her as soon as possible. She could read between the lines and knew her time with Jack was over. Vice President Lambkin was still suspicious of the President, but would wait for the right time to accuse him. The Chief of Staff, Richard Merrill, was by now totally engulfed with

Nora Prinston and wanted her no matter what. He would make his move when the time was right. Jack, however, had been in much prayer as to how he should proceed with his confessions and dealings with those who deserved his openness.

*

Nora was in the family quarters waiting on Jack to have lunch with her. Since Jack had been more attentive, she started to think that maybe they could make a go of it.

The Chief Butler brought in the lunch meal just as the President entered the dinning room. "Good afternoon, Mr. President, I hope you are having a nice day."

"Good afternoon, William. Thank you, and yes, I am having a nice day. I hope you are having one also?" William was a properly dressed man with impeccable manners, diction, and decorum.

Jack walked over to Nora, who by now was seated, and gazing at Jack. Jack bent down and gave Nora a lasting kiss on her neck, which she obviously welcomed by arching her back.

"And, how is your day, my love?" Jack said with his full attention on Nora.

The meal went well, and Jack and Nora spent the time talking about old fun things which brought up emotions that caressed both of their memories and inner desires. It was then that Jack asked Nora to come into the living room. He knew Rebecca was with friends someplace off the grounds and Nathan

182

was with Susan someplace. They were alone as they could be in the family quarters.

"Nora, I have something very important to tell you. I'm sure by now you have noticed some changes in me, or at least I hope you have noticed. Nevertheless, what I have to tell you may shock you, but I hope you will see the good in it." Jack was nervous, but managed to slowly advance the subject of his new found faith in God.

"Well, Jack, I have noticed some changes, and I welcome them. What has come over you?" Nora didn't want to spoil his momentum and let him talk.

"Nora, there are many wrong things in my life. I have made some terrible mistakes, some that have affected many lives. Things, that when you find them all out will shock you, disappoint you and probably repulse you. For the time being, however, let it suffice to say there are many revelations that will come out." Nora looked puzzled and thought to herself *"I can't imagine that there are too many things I don't know about, as he has been a very bad boy."*

Jack went on. "Nora about two months ago I turned my life over to God. It is as simple as that, a complete surrender to His lordship and control!" Nora's chin dropped opening her mouth with a 'what?' expression and a wild confused look. She said, "You did what?"

"I have turned my life over to God! I am a new man and I hope I am becoming a better man each day."

Nora tried to say something, but Jack stopped her and went on.

"Nora, I have been a terrible husband to you and a worse father to our children. I know you and I had our 'arrangement,' but it was wrong and I do not want it any more, I want only you!" Jack had tears in his eyes and waited for Nora to respond.

"Oh, Jack, I don't want the arrangement any more either. Can we start over?

"Yes, my love we can, with God's help! It won't be easy, but if we try we will succeed and be the stronger for it." What Jack forgot in this exciting exchange of human love was Nora's lack of understanding of what Jack had really done with and about God. Nora was very far removed from true spiritual understanding and only had knowledge of God through the many mediums that she consulted.

Jack being new at the honesty stuff was swept off his feet and felt like enough had been said. Nora and he were on new footing and the rest would come in time.

They hugged, kissed, and spent another hour talking and enjoying their re-kindled relationship.

When it came time for Jack to go back to the office he said, "Honey, I have to go, but we will pick this up later. Even though this is a fresh start there will be times of testing and I must confess other things to many people. Please be patient and give time for healing." He left for other encounters.

*

"Jane, I think the Vice-President is in the White House. Would you track him down and ask him to come by my office as soon as he can?" the President stated over the intercom as he shifted his weight in the plush, leather chair that had been passed down from President Kennedy.

Jack knew it was time to begin his confessions, and the Vice-President, who had been the recipient of much belittling, should be the first person to ask forgiveness from. Even the usual comfort of Kennedy's chair could not ease the soreness of his soul and mind. Although this road he was embarking on would lead to who knew where, it still had to be traveled. Just then Jane intercomed that the Vice-President had been found and he was waiting.

"Please ask him to come in."

John Lambkin had noticed Jack's change, but was cautious as to his motives and degree of demands. Lambkin was accustomed to the President putting demands on him that were only used to keep him quiet or to get him away from important decisions; however, lately he had been given important projects and was sincerely asked for his input. But, still, Jack could be setting him up to be the fall-guy for a dirty deal.

"Please come in, John. I hope I didn't interrupt what you were doing. I have some very important things that I must share with you and I have been putting it off for too long. Please have a seat." Jack tried to be as warm and outgoing as possible to make Lambkin feel welcomed.

"No, sir, I was finished with what I had to do, just as Jane Dean got in contact with me. What's up?" Lambkin kindly replied to Jack's obvious nervous, but seemingly genuine remarks.

"Well, John, I really don't know where to start, but first let me say how very sorry I am of the way I have treated you over the last few years. You are a man of integrity, and I have brushed your honesty aside many times." Jack was fidgeting with his ring and squirming in his chair.

"But, Mr. President, I, oh, I mean, what? Yes, you have, but maybe, well...I really don't know what to say!" is all Lambkin could say.

"John, you don't have to say anything. It is I who owe you an explanation. My attitude toward you and my condescending approach to your manhood is without excuse, and I truly apologize. Please forgive me!" Jack stood to his feet and walked to Lambkin with his hand out in a gesture of acceptance.

"Well, sir, I must say I never in my wildest dreams would have thought we would have a conversation such as this. I do forgive you. What has come over you, Jack?"

"I promise you there will be more revelations in the near future, but for now please be assured you have my full confidence and support in all areas, no matter what!" At that he gently ushered Lambkin to the door, who, happily surprised, went along like his name implied, a lamb.

Jack knew that since he had started the confessions he must forge ahead with Jane. He intercomed Jane and asked her to step into his office.

As Jane entered, with pen and pad, she commented on the Vice-President's demeanor. "Mr. President, whatever you said to the Vice-President sure made a new man out of him. He left here whistling and smiling from ear to ear."

"That's great Jane; I hope you will feel the same after you leave here today, as well!" Jack felt like this was going to be easy.

"Jane, I am sorry for the way I have treated you. I have played with your heart and left you stranded when I should not have. Please forgive me! My affections for you should not have taken the course they did, and I will do my best to insure they do not make me lose sight of what is important in our relationship." Jack was speaking truth, but missing the point and not able to express what was in his heart. Jane was getting the wrong impression!

"Oh, Jack, I understand, please say no more. I have noticed how you have changed of late, but I must say some of it is strange. But nevertheless, I will do my best as well to make things right!" She was about to go around Jack's desk and fall into his arms just as there was a knock on the door. She stopped!

"Come in!" Jack said, but happy that the mood had been broken.

Rebecca opened the door and barged in.

"Hi, Daddy, may I speak with you?" Rebecca had been basking in Jack's new found acceptance of his daughter and wanted to be around more than ever before. She even seemed to be calmer and in control of her faculties since Jack had been saved.

"Yes, sweetheart, come in!" he invited. Turning to his secretary, he dismissed her saying. "I'm sorry, Jane; we will talk more of this later, if you don't mind?" At that Jane left his office, smiling, feeling freer and thinking she and Jack were an item again.

Rebecca moved around the desk and sat on the edge as close to her father as possible. Jack didn't mind his daughter's attention now that he understood more of the spiritual side of human nature and those things that could affect it. He was cautious, however, and reached deep within his mind and soul to be as fatherly and lovingly as possible.

"Daddy, I still feel like many people around here do not like me. I hear people make comments about me when they don't know I'm listening; and it hurts!" She was the same old Rebecca who needed help, but Jack had other things that must be addressed before he could see to his daughter's freedom from mental anguish and demon control. He had no intention of locking her away as he had before and genuinely planned on helping her after the marriage of Nathan and Susan and his revelations to everyone. How he would do this was in question, as he wasn't sure what freedoms he would have after the revelations. Time would tell!

"Sweetie, I want you to know that you are very special to me, and I want to help you have peace of mind. You must find within yourself the strength to accept love from those who know you best. Your mother and I love you." Jack was stroking his daughter's face with one hand and smoothing her hair with the other. Rebecca responded to Jack's hands and calmed down to the point that she looked and sounded normal.

"Yes, Daddy, I know I must be calm, trust you, and find acceptance within myself. I know I need some help to make corrections and become level. Would you help me Daddy?" Rebecca's plea caused a small tear to well up in Jack's eyes and he looked away as he pulled his daughter into his arms. She felt loved and secure for the first time in many, many years.

"I tell you what, sweetheart; I'll be leaving office pretty soon and we'll spend a lot of time together.

We'll get some help and you'll get better, I promise!" Jack was being truthful and from his heart he made his mind up to follow through.

"Becky, you go find something happy to do, as I must get back to some other very important matters; OK?"

"OK, Daddy, I'll see you later...bye!" At that Rebecca was out the door, walking the straightest she had done in years, genuinely smiling without the trace of weirdness; you could almost say she had the resemblance of someone who was sane.

*

Jack intercomed Jane and asked her to get in contact with Lora Warner and ask her to come by for an appointment.

When Jane heard Lora's name coming from Jack's voice she was livid, but kept her composure and professionalism. She complied and called Lora.

Lora arrived just after lunch.

*

Rebecca was so happy with her new found relationship with her father that she couldn't help commenting on it to Jane as she passed her desk. "My daddy loves me, Jane, my daddy loves me!" was the excitable comment made to Jane as she wiped her hands across her desk.

As Rebecca got outside of Jane's office, just around the corner she stopped and leaned against the wall which was her accustomed departure from that office.   In the past it was to listen for any signs of negative comments, but this time it was just to stop and embrace the thoughts that made her happy over her father.   What she heard this time, although she was mistaken and it was all taken out of context, brought back the madness, but with murderous intentions.

What she heard, just before Jack asked Jane to call Lora Warner, was for Jane to get in contact with Dr. Livingston Morehouse.   Dr. Morehouse was a nationally known psychologist who was an expert in the matters of multiple personalities and deep depression.

Rebecca heard her father, over Jane's intercom say, "Jane, please get in contact with Dr. Livingston Morehouse at Wilburn Psychiatric Hospital and ask him if he would speak to me about my daughter." Jack's request was for knowledge and education in helping Rebecca, but Rebecca took it to mean that her father had been lying and was really going to have her committed. She would never know the truth!

*

After Lora Warner arrived, Jack asked her to come to the coffee room just outside his office. He was trying to make what he had to say as easy as possible and being in an open area would keep it safe for him and Lora. His good intentions, but naiveté, produced for others wrong results, but brought about the intended results with Lora.

"Lora, I'm so happy you agreed to come see me. I'm sorry that I have ignored you and left you hanging about our relationship." Lora knew that it was over, long before she was asked to come see Jack. She wasn't fooled and understood from Jack's silence over the past few months that their relationship was over. She put her right index finger over his mouth to silence him and said; "Jack, I know it's over with us. I have seen the change in your life and understand something profound has happened to you. I have known other people who have had similar changes and it can only be one thing...you have had some sort of religious experience and I understand! Please know that I wish you well and hope for your best!" Lora then gave Jack a gentle, but guarded hug, a kiss on the cheek, looked longingly into eyes and walked away smiling.

*

Nora was so happy with her rekindled relationship with Jack that she just had to go flirt with him at his office. She came through the executive office area by means of the side corridor which protects anyone from seeing who is traveling in that area. Just as she turned the corridor and peered into the coffee room alcove she saw Lora kiss Jack on the cheek. That kiss, innocent as it may have been, became the foundation for murder that would not be dissuaded no matter what. She turned without saying a word or making a sound and scampered back in the direction of the family quarters. But just as she was ascending the stairs she met Richard and fell into his arms.

Her soft, sobbing, firm grasp of Richard's arm, and weak, wobbling walk was all Richard needed to make him a man, at least in his own mind.

"What's the matter, Nora?"

"Oh, that Jack! I thought everything was right between us! Man, was I a fool! All he does is play me for a fool and break my heart. I wish he were dead!"

"Now, Nora, you don't mean that!"

"Yes, I do Richard. Yes, I do!"

"Nora, let's go someplace and calm down and talk about this!"

Richard and Nora found an empty hallway and talked. Richard was trying to calm Nora down, but in his heart he was deathly mad at Jack for hurting the only real woman he had ever loved. Nora, on the other hand, had had enough and found nothing in her heart for her husband but contempt, hate and darkness.

*

Jane knew that Jack and Lora were in his office and had no idea that they had gone to the coffee room just off his office. She was disturbed with Lora being with Jack alone and her jealousy caused her to check in on them. Her plan would be to go to the coffee room to see if she could hear anything going on in his office between them.

Her timing could not have been any worse as she turned the corner just in time to see Lora kiss Jack on the cheek. She was furious and stepped back in disgust. She was hurt and wounded and lost any control she had over sanity and reason.

Chapter

≈14≈

Jack in his honest approach to make amends to everyone was naively making things worse. His heart was right and his motives were pure, but his timing and wisdom in locations were turning his openness into a recipe for blood.

However Jack saw it and no matter what would be the outcome, he was determined to follow through with his confessions. Although he was extremely happy that Nathan was marrying Susan and they were Christians like himself now, he knew he had to tell them of his past no matter what that would do to their future. He surmised that love and honesty would be the best foundation for everyone.

It was late that evening that he asked Nathan and Susan to meet him in the "Secret Room." He knew they both knew of the room and it seemed to be the most appropriate place to confess his sins.

Nathan was excited as they went down to the basement to the one special place on earth that meant so much to them both. He couldn't contain himself as they approached the bookshelf that concealed the secret room. As he lifted the shelf and pulled it up and over, he gave out a little squeal and tugged on Susan's arm.

"Come on Susan, let's go in. Quickly!"

"Calm down, calm down! You will let everyone know where this place is," she said as her sense of adventure was lost in the reality and confession of her father before he died.

"Where is your sense of adventure? Aren't you the least bit excited about what dad wants to tell us?"

"Yes, but I can assure you that it isn't worth revealing this place to everyone!" *Unbeknownst to Nathan, Susan's disgust for Nathan's father was deep, and it made her skin crawl thinking about him and his lying lifestyle. It was no wonder that her "sense of adventure" wasn't there.* Just then Jack appeared in the door and walked in.

"Hi guys, how you doing?" Jack asked as he pulled the door closed and heard the shelf fall down and into place, leaving them alone and out of sight of any passersby.

"Hey, Dad, what's all the secrecy about? We aren't in trouble are we?" Nathan and Susan moved to the couch at Jack's request, and he took the one lone chair next to the wall.

"I want you both to know how happy I am that you are marrying. Susan, I couldn't think of a better wife for Nathan than you. Also, now that you are a Christian makes things even that much greater. You both must know that I approve of your marriage and pray for you daily." Jack was fidgeting a little with this kind of talk, but it felt good nevertheless.

"I'm going to tell you some things that will hurt you, I'm sure, and probably really make you think much less of me. Nevertheless, I have to do this; I have to confess things to you so that you do not hear it from others. I now know, since I have made Jesus my Lord, that honesty, confession, and repentance is not an option for a child of God, it is demanded!"

"Man, Dad, you are making me nervous, what could possibly be so dark that would make us think less of you?" Nathan was getting worried at his father's serious approach to this meeting.

"Well, son, what I have to tell you both will cause me to be removed from the Presidency and rightly so. It will bring embarrassment to our family and probably many people. It will upset our government and bring about many changes and cause people to question the Presidency in general. But, first I want to tell you how and when I turned my life over to Jesus!" At the mention of Jesus Jack's whole demeanor changed and his faced softened, his hands stopped shaking, and he generally looked like a happier man.

He went on to tell Nathan and Susan about his conversion and how it had touched his life and whole being. He expounded upon the moment with Nathan and that day in the swimming pool and how he was touched by Nathan's questions and the inner tug of his need for God. He shared about the women, crooked deals that got him into office and general life decisions that made him who he was. Then he came to the part about Senator Hanson, the money and people who were killed because of his greed and desire for power.

"Susan, what I am going to say next will hurt you very much. It involves your dad," Jack said to Susan as he focused on her eyes.

"What do you mean, my dad?

"I knew him really before you did." said Jack softly.

"What? How did you know him?" is all she said.

"I read the Washington Post every morning. When I read the obituaries, I noticed that a Darrell Collins had been murdered in his car. After checking him out I realized he was the man I had hired to do things for me. I also checked his history and found out that he was your father. I didn't talk to you about it because I was afraid at that time you would find out what I am going to tell you now." Jack was squirming in his seat.

"Do you both remember Senator Hanson and his death?" They nodded affirmatively.

"Well, I hired Darrell Collins to kill Senator Hanson and those associated with him and me in the money stealing deal." Jack said it fast like he was hoping it would sound less terrible.

"Come on, Dad, you aren't serious are you?" Nathan exclaimed, not wanting to believe anything he was hearing. "Surely you are kidding us and just making things up?"

Susan didn't say a word through the whole confession and then she slowly spoke up.

"Mr. President…" Jack cut her off.

"Please, Susan, call me Jack!"

She in turn cut him off and calmly spoke, "Mr. President, I know everything," as she began to cry.

"What?" said Nathan.

"What?" said Jack.

"Yes. I know the whole gory mess and damnable details. My father told me the night he was killed."

"What? You didn't know your dad," said Nathan with surprise.

"I didn't. I mean I didn't know him before the night he died. He knew he was dying from a gun shot wound, and I was called to meet him so he could tell me what he had done before he died. The so-called robbery murder was a setup by him so I wouldn't be asked a bunch of questions about him being shot at my apartment."

"Whaaat?" is all Nathan could say.

Susan went on to explain her knowledge of her father's involvement and his association with the President and how he was shot and died.

"I am so sorry, Susan. Son, I am so sorry," Jack sputtered through tears as he said those words.

Susan turned to Nathan and said, "Nathan, I'm sorry I didn't tell you before. I didn't know how to tell you. I was trying to figure out what to do. I told you I was going on a newspaper business trip but in reality I went to Georgia to bury my father."

Nathan's mouth dropped and then he said, "Boy, am I in the dark."

"I'm sorry Nathan, I should have told you."

"But, Dad, how could you? I mean, why? Man, am I confused!" Nathan's words hit Jack deeply and tears began to slide down his cheek.

"I know that this is very difficult for you both, and I know it makes your new life together start off with darkness, but I can't run from my life and the effects it has had on people. I am so very sorry for all of this and ask you for forgiveness; PLEASE!" Jack's face was completely wet now with tears, and his shirt looked like someone had thrown a bucket of water on him.

Nathan reached out to his father, wrapped his arms around Jack's neck and began to cry also.

Susan sat looking at Nathan and his father holding each other and crying. Because her emotions were going crazy, her love for Nathan and her understanding of Jack's confession was too much, she reached in and cried with them.

Susan then said softly, "I forgive you!"

There they were, a father who in the past wouldn't hug, a son who didn't know the touch of a loving father, but now both realizing what genuine compassion and love were, and a confused girl learning the hard way what forgiveness demands. It was a beginning and an ending all in one. The beginning of their love for each other, and end because Jack would probably spend time in prison, and away from those who had come to know him in a different way.

Jack revealed more, but soon came to a point where everything that he had to say was said and the three of them were exhausted.

"Nathan, Susan, I don't know what else to say, but one thing I know we must do is pray!" They huddled together, grasping each other's shoulders, touching as closely as possible and prayed.

"Dad, what are you going to do?" Nathan asked after the prayer.

"Well, son, I am going to contact the Attorney General and confess my sins. From there it is in God's hands!"

Their encounter lasted four hours and they departed

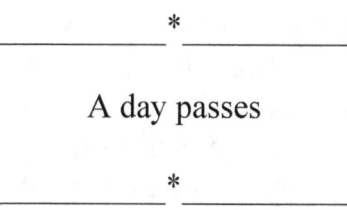

The stage had been set, demons had taken control of willful minds, and innocent people had been hurt. But, in another sense things had been made right. Jack was now a good man for his surrender to God. But that didn't excuse his murderous dealings and sinful ways to mankind. These deeds had to be paid for.

Jack told no one else of his life and dark dealings and spent most of the time forming his words and confession that would be spoken to the Attorney General; he planned the next day to make a full disclosure to him.

It was about 7 PM and everyone had departed the White House for the day. Jack knew that Jane had said goodbye for the day earlier and didn't act as if there were any problems. Nora was supposedly in the residence. Nathan and Susan were off someplace making marriage arrangements at his insistence. Rebecca was probably doing her crazy wandering around, and the White House in general was quiet.

Jack felt it would be the perfect time to go to the "Secret Room" and pray.

As he left his office, he told Agent Whitaker that he would be unavailable for a short while and for the agent to stand near the stairs to the family quarters and that he would be there in about thirty minutes. This request was not out of the ordinary lately as he was in the habit since his conversion to pray, and the White House staff didn't disturb him nor try to find him.

He made his way down the stairs, through the dusty halls, past the furnace and into the room which contained the secret shelves that would open the "Secret Room," which by now had been christened by Jack as the "Prayer Room."

Knowing what was going to happen tomorrow should have given Jack cause for great concern, but oddly he was calm and peaceful. Taking the time to pray seemed to be the best thing in his life now. It put everything in perspective and made the world go away for awhile. It seemed that nothing could cloud his joy when he was in the presence of God through prayer.

He entered the room and went right to the one lone chair in the room, knelt down and began to pray. He left the door open this time as he was in a hurry to come into the throne room of the Most High.

As soon as he began to pray he felt a terrible weight on his shoulders. It was greater than anything he had ever felt before in his short time as a praying man. It even scared him somewhat and made him hunker down as he prayed.

Someplace in that room he could hear what seemed to be very soft, but gruff voices trying to dissuade him from prayer. He had never realized this before in prayer and even opened his eyes to see if anyone was there. There was no one to be seen!

As he prayed on, his mind became clear, his resolve to be concise with God became center, and his love for others cascaded over everything and everyone he ever knew. It seemed that love was the most important thing in the entire universe at that moment. As usual, he confessed his sins again; he knew he had been forgiven, but it just seemed to be right when you were dealing with a loving God.

"Oh, God, I thank you for loving and forgiving me. Thank you that my future is in your hands. I don't know what tomorrow will bring, but I know you know tomorrow. Please help me to do what I must do. Help me to be patient and kind to everyone. Let others see you in me. Even though they may see the Devil, I want them to see you!" Jack could somewhat relate to Jesus as he prayed in the Garden the night of His arrest.

Jack didn't hear anyone coming or he would have gotten up and shut the door to the room, but by the time he did notice, it was too late.

*

Nathan and Susan were beside themselves with the knowledge of Jack's revelations; Susan loved Nathan without any reservations, but she also knew that some how it would make a difference in their relationship.

Obviously, they put their wedding plans on hold and spent many hours in prayer seeking the right course of action and how to proceed with marriage.

Late on the second day of Jack's confessions they met to discuss the matter. They decided to go to the Dark Roast coffee shop to discuss it.

The booth they sat in on their first meeting didn't seem to be too special now as it was overcast with the knowledge of murder, prison for Dad, and the general confusion of Nation's response when revealed.

"Susan, I am so confused and just don't know what to do!"

"Nathan, you must trust the Lord and lean on his guidance and understanding!" Susan responded as she touched and caressed his hand.

"I know, but you just don't understand, I must do something! It wouldn't be right to sit back and let Dad take on this whole thing by himself!"

"Well, honey, there really isn't anything you or anyone else can do, as this must be walked out by your Dad, because it is his doing and not yours!" Susan's response wasn't meant to point blame or to dismiss Nathan's love and concern for his dad, but just a common sense approach to what must be done.

"Now, wait a minute, Susan, I know that Dad is the cause of this whole ugly thing, but he needs my support and love! After all, he has confessed, he's a Christian now, and he needs us! Don't you think so?" Nathan's attitude took on a defensive tone, but without realizing where it could lead.

"If we don't stand by my Dad, he has no one to give him support in the darkest time of his life! We can't stand back and just say 'It's his bed now he has to lie in it!' I won't do that, Susan, and I don't care what you say!" Nathan's voice was raised and somewhat shrill and drew the attention of those sitting in other booths.

Nathan's tone, mannerism, and body language was like putting a red flag in front of a bull in the ring; it brought out in Susan her competitive nature and the old person in her that loved a fight. She responded without thinking and quietly blurted back at Nathan "Well, it is his fault, and now everyone else will suffer for his stupid mistakes!"

"Well, that's really the way to look at it, Susan. Some kind of forgiving Christian you are! Why don't you just go kick him in the ribs right now?" Nathan's face was red and a little tear began walking its way down his check.

Susan realized that her outburst, which came from her own confusion and frustration, was wrong, tried to take back her stupid words. But no matter what she said, it couldn't put the right size bandage on the wound she had just inflected upon Nathan's ego and hurt. But, she tried!

"Nathan, I didn't mean that! I was responding out of my own frustration and hurt. Please forgive me!"

"Susan, I think we need a break. Maybe we need to take some time and regroup our thoughts and where we stand!" Nathan slowly spoke out this reply, but very calmly and with a steel eyed glare. He then slowly slid out of the booth and began to walk toward the door.

"Nathan, please don't leave. Let's talk. I am truly sorry. We both need to just calm down and figure out what to do!" Susan's words were there, but they fell on a hurt ego, a confused soul, and someone who didn't want to believe that the very thing he had craved from his dad: namely affection and acceptance, which might now be taken away. His hurt wouldn't let him see the need for self control and cooler thinking! He just slowly walked away.

Susan's new world was unraveling before her eyes, and she had no grasp for the moment of any power that would keep it cemented together. All she could do was stay seated and softly cry.

*

Richard Merrille, like everyone else, knew that Jack was going down to the basement often and knew where to find him.

"Richard?" said Jack with a surprise! "What are you doing here?"

"Jack, I have had enough of your crooked dealings and low life antics. It's time someone did something about your lying mouth. Also, the way you have treated Nora is beyond even you! I hated you for years for taking Nora from me in college, but I put up with it until now. I will have her no matter what!" Richard was standing there with a pistol pointed right at Jack's mouth.

Just then Jane Dean stepped into the room. Richard was startled, but did not change his composure nor lower the gun.

Jane didn't seem to mind that Richard was there and began a verbal tirade at Jack. "How could you play with my heart? You led me on, giving me hope and then letting me down with that tramp Lora. I hate you Jack! You deserve to die!" At the word die she reached into her purse and pulled out a little twenty two revolver and pointed it at Jack's heart.

If this scene wasn't so dangerous it would have been funny. Richard standing there with his jaw down looking at Jane and his gun pointed at Jack's mouth. Jane's words seeming to flow out of her mouth and almost tangibly hitting Jack. You could write books about this stuff! And if that weren't enough, Nora came running into the room with a gun of her own and pointed it at Jack's hand.

"Nora, what are you doing; what are you all doing! Are you all nuts?" is all Jack could say. "What is going on?"

Nora too, didn't seem to mind the other two, would be assassins, and began her verbal poisonous attack of Jack. "You dirty, lying, loveless loser Jack! How could you touch that filthy Lora? You said you loved me and wanted things to work between us. How could you? You sure know how to reach into someone's heart and manipulate as you want! But when I saw you touching and kissing that little tramp, that did it; I'll make sure you don't touch her again." With that she raised her gun and took aim at Jack's right hand.

Before Nora could pull the trigger they all heard someone running down the hall, screaming like a Tasmanian devil, the cartoon character. The screamer turned out to be Rebecca.

Rebecca came running into the room gun in hand and pointed it at her father's head. "You will not have me committed to a crazy house, Daddy. You lied to me, you said you would help and not have me committed. You think you are so smart, but I'll show you who is crazy. You are crazy if you think I will go to the nut house!" Rebecca looked totally different with her face distorted, her hands trembling, and with jerky movements. She obviously was not in control.

Rebecca was not aware of the others in the room. In general they all seemed to not recognize that there were other humans in the room other than Jack.

Also, no one seemed to hear the voices that came from the very air that were screaming for death. In the confusion being able to distinguish between sane voices and the guttural sounds of demonic madness was impossible. Only Jack could distinguish between them, but the other four were in their own little mad hurricane world.

"Daddy, you are dead!" Rebecca screamed and took aim at Jack's head, but stopped from pulling the trigger.

"Becky, stop, you don't know what you are doing. Let me help you!" With the words 'Let me help you!' you could hear the devilish voices scream *"Kill him, kill him, pull the trigger! Do it now!"* And with the 'Do it now!' all four pulled the trigger.

Jack fell forward onto his knees as if he were in prayer. He was dead!

The four wild and crazed murderers heard the gun shots, but didn't realize that they as individuals had pulled their gun trigger. They only saw the results and looked startled. Each in turn quickly left the room and fled into their own confused world.

The sardonic laughter of the unseen beings could be heard just above the fading echoes of gun shots. Although their form could not be realized in the small, one bulb lit room, they were there nevertheless. After the shots that ripped through flesh, shattered bone, and ended a life, the demons were pleased with their convincing demands on open minds of madness.

Upon hearing gun shots coming from the basement area, Agent Whitaker came running down the stairs. He passed the four dazed assassins as each ran willy-nilly up the stairs. As he ran, he shouted and asked what had happened, but none of the glassy eyed murderers seemed to notice his presence on the stairs.

Upon arriving in the death room, Whitaker found the President dead. He was found on his knees in a praying position, but seemed to be smiling.

The agent tried to revive the President after calling for help but to no avail. The President was dead!

*

It didn't take long before Nora, Rebecca, Jane and Richard were caught. None of them tried to hide their deed; Nora and Rebecca confessed as soon as the FBI came into the family quarters to inform them of Jack's death.

After they had fired their weapons and left the room they went to the family quarters, sat at the dining table and held each others hands. Rebecca was like a zombie and Nora was in a daze. They quietly spoke of their hurt and dismay over Jack's actions that led up to the shots.

Jane was waiting at home with a new dress she had bought the day before the murder. She too just spoke of Jack's indiscretions.

Richard Merrill was found sitting in his office quietly writing instructions for his staff with things that had to be done. He didn't repent nor did he seem to be sorry. He just said "It had to be done, and I love Nora!"

Nathan and Susan grieved deeply for Jack and for her father. They got back together at the funeral and walked behind the caisson carrying the President's body to Arlington Cemetery.

They waited a week after the funeral to tell the Attorney General of Jack's confession about the "Green Paper" deal and the many deaths and the people involved.

The Attorney General didn't hold them for anything because he knew the family had suffered enough, and besides, everyone who was a part of the whole thing was dead. What was left of the stolen money was recovered and sent back to the treasury for destruction.

The nation was never told of the "Green Paper" theft. The media reported that the President had been killed by confused and angry people in his life; that because of his many affairs with women, his wife, and love interest secretary had plotted to kill him; that his daughter, who was mentally ill and confused, agreed to help kill her father; that Richard Merrill had allowed his long-festering jealousy lead him to murder.

Nora, Richard and Jane were given life sentences for the murder because they knowingly and willingly knew the difference between right and wrong.

Rebecca was sent to a hospital for the criminally insane, where she would probably live out the rest of her days.

Vice-President Lambkin became President and made real, honest changes that helped the nation. He found his own place of leadership and quickly stepped into authority without self intimidation.

Albert Frank, the plumber became close friends with Nathan and Susan, and they met often. Albert became a fulltime minister and a spiritual adviser to the young Prinstons.

Poker Player was never told that the man he had shot at Susan's apartment that night was her father or that he had died. With Susan's encouragement, Poker Player became a certified private detective in Washington, D.C.

Oh, and about Jack? What wasn't realized by anyone in that one bulb lit room that evening was the figure that stepped out of this existence and into another. It was Jack!

You see, God promises that if anyone is in Christ Jesus, he becomes a new person and if he is absent from his body, he will be present with the Lord! Jack's body wasn't fit for eternity, but his soul was!

You may ask, what about Jack's life and sins? Well, they were terrible, but they came under the blood of the One who paid for all sinners' dark life: Jesus!

The Beginning of a new life!